THE LEGEND OF SNOWDEER, PLUM PUDDIN' & PURPLE MOUSE

BY RANDY PLUMMER

Copyright © 2018

Randy Plummer
Plum Puddin' Productions

This is a work of fiction. Actual people, places, companies, and products are mentioned to give the book more of a sense of reality, but all dialogue and incidents contained in this book are the product of the author's imagination.

DEDICATION

I want to dedicate this third story in the SNOWDEER® series to my parents, Darrell & Rose Marie Plummer. GOD bless You Mom & Daddy. I love you! You were among those who created the tradition and excitement of live music shows in Branson when you debuted the Plummer Family Country Music Show in 1973. Your legacy continues to this day in each of the shows and entertainers that have followed in your footsteps. Your music and creative genius lives on in the recordings you left us, and also in the stories of Snowdeer, created by your prodigy and biggest fan. To honor you, I've included a picture of your 1985 induction into the Ozarks Music Hall of Fame in Branson, MO.

CONTENTS

ARTIST'S CONCEPTION OF SNOWDEER CHARACTERS

SNOWDEER
Sarah ("Starry") Martin – 2018

TASHA MOUSE
Tasha Dunne – 2018

PLUM PUDDIN' & PINECONE
Sarah ("Starry") Martin – 2018

PINECONE
Sarah ("Starry") Martin – 2018

CARROTT RABBIT "LOGO"
Sarah ("Starry") Martin – 2018

CARROT THE RABBIT
Sarah ("Starry") Martin – 2018

1 - SNOWDEER GETS SNOWBALLED

Once upon a time, Snowdeer, Plum Puddin', Purple Mouse and their friends were playing in the snow in the Possum Holler Woods over by Knob Lick. Ka-Boom! Smack dab on the back of Plum Puddin's head, Snowdeer throws a big snowball! He also throws one at Pinecone, Plum Puddin's dog, but he misses and then watches as Pinecone runs to hide behind a big cedar tree.

Plum Puddin' turns around to Snowdeer and hollers, "Ok, two can play that game!"

Then Plum Puddin says to Pinecone, "Stand back 'ole boy and watch this!"

He looks at Snowdeer and says, "You don't know who you're messin' with when you start a snowball fight with me!"

"Oh, you think so?" asks Snowdeer.

"Yeah, you ain't had a snowball fight till you've fought with the Plum!" jokes Plum Puddin'. Then Plum Puddin' bends over and starts gathering snow to make a large snowball to throw at Snowdeer. While he is still bent over gathering snow, he feels a snowball hit him on his shoulder. Then another. And then another! Plum Puddin' can't see Snowdeer because of all of the snowballs that are headed his way!

"What are you using over there, a cannon?" asks Plum Puddin' laughing.

"Nope," says Snowdeer. "I use all four legs!" Then Snowdeer turns his back to Plum Puddin' and starts making snowballs and then goes bucking and kicking the snowballs at Plum Puddin'. He keeps going until Plum Puddin' is laying on the ground covered in snow and shouting, "I give up! You win!" Then, all of a sudden, Snowdeer feels a snowball on his back. Then another. And then the snowballs really start flying at him! When he looks around, he sees Purple Mouse, Todd Lott and his horse Glister, Terrie Young Deer, Pastor Donn, Gaylene, Niangua & Taneycomo throwing snowballs at him. "Oh no!" exclaims Snowdeer and they playfully give Snowdeer the snowball fight of his life!

After a little while, Terrie Young Deer says, "We'd better stop because we're liable to bury Snowdeer so deep in snow that we'd never find him till spring!"

They all laugh and Plum Puddin' says to Todd Lott, "Hey Todd, let's go pull Snowdeer out of the snow and then would you please let us use your sleigh and have Glister pull us over to my cabin? I'll make us some hot chocolate and warm up some Plum Pudding and then we can all sit around the fireplace and visit."

Todd nods and says, "Yea Plum, I'd be happy to do that. I'm ready to get out of this snow and sit in front of a nice warm fire!" So, they all load up on Todd's sleigh and bundle up close together in quilts.

1

Purple Mouse looks at Todd and asks, "Can we take a different path and go through Buckhorn please? It's a closer route to Plum Puddin's cabin, and I'm freezing!"

"Sure," answers Todd as he grabs the reins. Then he says, "Giddy up Glister, let's go to Plum Puddin's cabin," and off Glister goes sleighing through the snow in a trot.

2 - DOSI DOE

As they are getting closer to Plum Puddin's cabin, Terrie Young Deer says, "Christmas is only 4 weeks away and Thanksgiving is this week."

"Yes, it's almost here Young Deer. What do you have planned for this year's celebration?" asks Plum Puddin'.

Terrie Young Deer answers, "I'm going to have the Thanksgiving meal in my tepee with Niangua and Taneycomo and serve turkey, corn meal cakes, pumpkin, squash and serve a big variety of nuts I have stored from the fall harvest. I try to live up to my Indian name, "Cornucopia" that you gave me Plum, and this year's harvest for sure gave me a horn of plenty!" And then she laughs.

Plum Puddin' joins her laughing and he says, "You always live up to your name."

Terrie Young Deer smiles and then gets an idea and says, "I want to invite you all to come Thanksgiving."

"Thank you, I will be there," says Plum Puddin' and all the others join in saying they will come too.

In a little bit, they come to Buckhorn and cross the ice on the Little Piney Creek. Pastor Donn says, "I always enjoy going through Buckhorn. I've seen more people saved here and then baptized in the Little Piney Creek than most anywhere."

"Good thing you're not baptizing today Brother Donn, 'cause they'd freeze solid before you got 'em out of the water and I know you don't want no Cold-hearted Christians, do you?" jokes Purple Mouse.

"Purple Mouse, they'd turn as purple as you do when you blush when you're looking at Tasha Mouse," jokes Gaylene.

After hearing that, Purple Mouse turns a deep purple color and looks down and shakes his head. The whole gang laughs and Purple Mouse says, "You all have me blushing so much that I'm gonna need to put some snow on my face to cool it off."

"Oh, we'd be happy to help you out with that," Plum Puddin' answers.

"No, no, I'm Ok. I don't need any help. I've seen how you put snow on faces," Purple Mouse replies and laughs.

As the gang continue sleighing through the Buckhorn forest, they happen to see something hiding behind some trees watching them. They see it jump quickly from tree to tree, but the trees are so close together they can't tell what it is. Snowdeer looks at Plum Puddin' and Plum Puddin' says, "Todd, would you please stop the sleigh? We have to know what that is hiding in the woods."

3

So Todd has Glister stop and Snowdeer, Plum Puddin' and Purple Mouse hop off the sleigh. As they walk through the snow, they try to see the mysterious figure. But every time they get close, It jumps behind another big tree farther away from them and then slinks down. Snowdeer, not wanting it to get away says, "Please, don't be afraid, we won't hurt you. Come out, we want to meet you." They watch as a beautiful young doe slowly makes her way through the tall cedar trees. "A deer!" says Snowdeer. Then he asks, "What's your name?"

The shy little doe looks at them and answers, "My name is Dosi Doe."

"Dosi Doe, what a beautiful name. Is this your home?" asks Snowdeer.

"No, I'm from Branson, she answers. I've lived there all my life, but I got lost in a snow storm and ended up here. Where are you all from?"

"We're from over Knob Lick, Possum Holler and Doe Run area," Snowdeer answers.

Then Plum Puddin' says, "It's nice to meet you Dosi Doe. My name is Plum Puddin'. Would you like to join us? We're riding over to my cabin at Possum Holler by Knob Lick. We're going to warm up by my fire and have hot chocolate and Plum Pudding and get a nice long visit in. We'd love to have you come along."

"Plum Puddin' and Plum Pudding?" asks Dosi Doe.

"Yes, my mama Rose Marie and Daddy Darrell named me after Plum Pudding because ever since I was a little baby I've loved it and I eat it all the time," Plum Puddin' says and laughs. Then it dawns on Plum Puddin' that he hadn't introduced everybody and he says, "Dosi Doe, this is Purple Mouse and Snowdeer."

Dosi Doe smiles and says, "Hello, it's a pleasure to meet you. Thank you all for rescuing me, I really appreciate it."

Then Snowdeer says, "You're welcome Dosi Doe, we're happy to help." Here's another great friend in the making, Plum Puddin' thinks to himself and Snowdeer says, "Let's go over to the sleigh Dosi Doe. I want to introduce you to all our other friends." So, they go back to the sleigh and Snowdeer introduces everyone to Dosi Doe. As they take off for Plum Puddin's cabin, Dosi Doe smiles to herself knowing that the good Lord has brought her path to cross with some great new friends.

3 - DOSI DOE AND BRANSON THE BALLADEER

As Dosi Doe and her new found friends are making their way through the Buckhorn woods, Pinecone goes over and lays down beside her and gives her a whimper and a nudge on her leg with his nose.

Dosi Doe laughs and says, "Who does he belong to?"

Plum Puddin' laughs and says, "I'm so sorry, I forgot to introduce you to my dog Pinecone. Sorry ole boy. Dosi Doe-meet Pinecone. Pinecone-meet Dosi Doe."

"Nice to meet you Pinecone," Dosi Doe says as she rubs one of her hooves on his head. Pinecone gets excited and gives a little bark and then lays his head on her leg.

Then Plum Puddin' tells Dosi Doe, "Pinecone and I go everywhere together and even at times when I go visitin' Santa at the North pole......oops!"

"What? I have to hear this story Plum Puddin'!" says Dosi Doe.

Knowing he let the cat out of the bag, Plum Puddin' says, "Ok, you may not believe me, but everyone here knows it's the truth. Me and Pinecone go to the North Pole and see Santa every year. Mr. and Mrs. Claus are friends of ours." All the gang in the sleigh laugh and tell her it's the truth and once again Pinecone gives a nudge on Dosi Doe's leg with his nose and gives out a little bark to let her know what Plum Puddin' is saying is true.

Then Plum Puddin' says, "Dosi Doe, here's my story...Once upon a time on Christmas Eve, I left Santa a jar of Plum Pudding for his Christmas present. He loved it so much that in turn, he left me a magical jar with a note that said whenever I wanted to go to the North Pole, all I had to do was hold the jar in my right hand and say the magical words, "HO-HO-HO! OFF TO THE NORTH POLE WE GO!" and Santa's magical Sugar Snow would sweep me and Pinecone up to the North Pole! While I am there I can visit Santa, Mrs. Santa, Harvey the Elf, Josh Elf, Amber Elf, Lilly Kay Elf , Ilsa Marie Elf and Branson The Balladeer and......"

Dosi Doe stops him and says, "Branson The Balladeer?"

"Yes, Branson The Balladeer. He has a great voice and has become a special friend," Plum Puddin' answers.

Dosi Doe then shouts, "I know him! We didn't know what happened to him! All my parents and I knew is that one year during a hard winter's snow, Branson went out to meet his forest friends and go Christmas Caroling. He got lost when the bad snowstorm hit. The snow was coming down so hard you couldn't see your hoof in front of your face and the wind made the snow pile up real high. We sent out a search party for him and covered forest after forest for weeks. We went to Garber, Reeds Spring, Blue Eye, Mountain Home, Pea Ridge, Ozark, Green Forest...I can't name them all-and none of us could find him! I still have been going out looking for him after all this time and I kept hoping and praying I might see him somewhere in these woods. I have wondered so many times if he was hurt in the forest and didn't remember where he was or wouldn't be able to walk to come home to Branson. Anyway, that's what I was doing when you found me-I was searching for him and I ended up getting lost! I'm so thankful you came by and that you're letting me go with you!"

Plum Puddin' wonders why she would be looking for him for such a long time and he asks, "Dosi Doe, how do you know Branson The Balladeer? Is he a friend or someone you sang with?"

Dosi Doe answers, "No, he's much more than that-He's my brother."

Everyone's mouth drops open as they learn this great news! Then Snowdeer says, "I can't believe he's your brother! We all love him and love to hear him sing! He's always writing songs too. Wait till we go back to the North Pole! We'll tell him and he can come back with us to see you!"

"Hey Snowdeer, why don't we take Dosi Doe to the North Pole to surprise him?" asks Plum Puddin'.

"What a Christmas present that would be," says Purple Mouse.

"Oh, yes! Please take me to see him-I would really appreciate it," says Dosi Doe.

Everyone agrees that taking her to the North Pole is a wonderful idea and Todd gets so excited to get back, that he tells Glister to giddy up faster! Glister picks up the pace and off they go to Plum Puddin's cabin to celebrate their new friend and plan their next trip to the North Pole so Dosi Doe can meet her brother, Branson The Balladeer.

4 - CABIN PLANS

As Todd and Glister pull the sleigh up to Plum Puddin's cabin, Dosi Does eyes fill with tears as she thinks how special this day has been. She can't wait to see the Homestead of her new friend Plum Puddin' and enjoy a night of fun with all of his friends. It's almost too overwhelming for her and not being able to hold it in any longer, she says, "I'm so thankful to God and to all of you for saving me out there in the forest and for telling me I will get to see my brother again! I can't thank you enough."

"That's what friends are for and we are thankful to have met you too Dosi Doe and to be your friends," says Plum Puddin' as he helps her off the sleigh. Then Plum Puddin' says to everyone, "Go on in the cabin. I'm gonna go get some extra firewood 'cause I think we're gonna be up for a while tonight," and then he laughs and heads to the woodshed.

By now, it's getting dark and Purple Mouse runs ahead of everyone and goes inside the cabin. They watch as the windows light up as Purple Mouse begins lighting lamps inside. When he comes back out, he's holding a lantern so they can see their way up to the cabin.

As they go in, Dosi Doe says, "Oh, what a beautiful cabin! It's so homey and warm!"

"Thank you," says Plum Puddin' as he comes through the back door with his arms full of firewood.

They hear something coming down the stairs and look over to see Purple Mouse's mother Orchid and his father Maroon. "Hello Y'all," they say.

Then Maroon says, "I see a new face!"

Then Orchid smiles at Dosi Doe and asks, "What's your name dear?"

Dosi Doe answers, "My name is Dosi Doe. It's nice to meet you all."

"Nice to meet you too Dosi Doe," they answer back.

Maroon goes on to tell Dosi Doe, "Plum Puddin' rescued us a long time ago when we were passing through Possum Holler. He gave us a place to stay because Orchid was going to give birth to Purple Mouse and we didn't have a home. He took us in and now we've become family and we live upstairs in this cabin. He said we can stay as long as we want and for that we are very thankful!"

"It looks like I'm not the only one who's been rescued by Plum Puddin'," says Dosi Doe laughing.

Then Plum Puddin' says, "Dosi Doe, you'll always have us for friends and a place to come visit right here. Once you're our friend, you're stuck with us forever! That is, if you want!"

They all laugh and talk way into the night with stories mostly being about Dosi Doe and Branson The Balladeer and Snowdeer, Plum Puddin' and Purple Mouse's travels to the North Pole.

Plum Puddin' gets a grin on his face and says, "Speaking of the North Pole..." and then he goes to the cupboard and brings out his magical jar that Santa gave him. Then he says to Dosi Doe, "This jar has taken me and Pinecone to the North Pole many, many times. I love it there so much! So much so that one Easter during Pastor Donn's sunrise church service, I got a notion to go to the North Pole and I left church early and came home and got this jar out of the cupboard. I put it in my right hand and said the magical words, "HO-HO-HO! OFF TO THE NORTH POLE WE GO!" and Pinecone and I celebrated Easter Sunday there!"

They all laugh and Pastor Donn says, "So, that's why you left church early! I thought it was because you wanted to skip putting anything in the offering plate."

Everyone laughs and Plum Puddin' says, "I had to see if the elves had painted Easter eggs and if there was any Easter candy there."

"Now you have me wondering, do they?" asks Terrie Young Deer.

"Yes, they sure do and Santa always celebrates this special Season. They stop their work and go to church and remember the Lord Jesus who is the reason for the Easter Season - just like they remember the Christmas Season - honoring when Jesus was born," says Plum Puddin'.

All the gang goes, "AHHHH" and Dosi Doe says, "I can hardly wait to go!"

Plum Puddin' continues saying, "You're gonna love it and there's so many more things we haven't even told tonight that Santa has up there! You won't believe your eyes! Plus, your brother is going to be there too! Snowdeer, Purple Mouse and I have enough stories of our North Pole adventures that we could write a book."

"That's for sure," Snowdeer and Purple Mouse agree. Then Snowdeer says, "Dosi Doe, just think. Soon you will be there and you will have your own stories to tell of your North Pole adventures."

Dosi Doe smiles real big and says, "Yes, and when I tell my Mama and Daddy all the stories, they will be so happy! And especially when I tell them about Branson The Balladeer, they will be brought to tears."

Plum Puddin' grins and says, "I'm so excited for you to get to go Dosi Doe. Your life will never be the same." Then, all of a sudden, Plum Puddin's grandfather clock strikes and shows 3am. Plum looks at the clock and laughs and says, "Time sure flies when you're talking about Santa and the North Pole! Oh well, let's go to bed and talk about it tomorrow. Everyone is welcome to stay the night here at the cabin. I'll make you all pallets to sleep on and I also have some extra featherbeds, so you can get a good night's sleep. Tomorrow, we'll make up plans for our next trip to see Santa after eating a good country breakfast with lots of Plum Pudding!" then he laughs again. He looks at Dosi Doe and says, "Dosi Doe, Tomorrow, I want to show you around this part of the Ozarks."

"I would love that Plum Puddin'," she answers.

Then, the rest of the gang says, "We want to go with you and show you where we live too."

Dosi Doe smiles and says, "I would love to see where you all live." So, they all hug and say their good nights and after settling into their pallets and featherbeds, Plum Puddin' blows out the lamps with a very thankful heart for all the good things the good Lord had done for them that day.

5 - PLUM PUDDIN'S BREAKFAST PRAYER

The next morning, they all wake up to the smell of bacon and eggs frying and homemade biscuits rising at the hearth. Plum Puddin' has already been up long before and had done the milkin', gathered the eggs, and fed Todd's horse Glister and his own horses Brownback and Charcoal, who is going to foal or in other words, going to give birth to a baby horse.

Plum Puddin' has almost everything ready for breakfast, so he hollers, "Everybody, get up! Breakfast is about ready!" and then he makes a sound like a rooster crowing at the dawning of the day. That makes everyone laugh, and one by one, they yawn and stretch and climb out of bed. Plum Puddin' goes over to the table and throws a big checkered table cloth on it. Then he goes and gets some jars of Plum Pudding and jelly and some honey butter to go with the bacon, eggs and biscuits.

"Good mornin' Y'all," says Plum Puddin', breaking the silence.

"Good morning Plum," they slowly answer back.

Then Plum says, "Come to the table and eat up." So, after they have all gathered at the table, Plum Puddin' says, "I'll say the prayer." Then he prays. "Dear Lord Jesus, Thank You for another day You've given to us. Thank You for our new friend Dosi Doe and please make it where soon she will get to see her brother Branson The Balladeer at the North Pole. O, and thank You for the food and bless it and make it where everyone will like it–just in case I didn't do a good job on it! In Jesus name I pray, Amen!"

And the rest say, "Amen" and then they start laughing.

Plum Puddin' sees them laughing, so he smiles and says, "Hey, God has a sense of humor and the Bible says in Proverbs 17:22 that laughter does good like a medicine."

Snowdeer laughs and says, "Yes, the good Lord said that for sure Plum, and I have no doubt that you'll be giving us a lot of your kind of medicine in the future!"

They all agree and give a hearty "AMEN", and then start digging into their breakfast that tasted just right.

6 - MANE IS BORN

Just as they are finishing up breakfast, they begin hearing loud noises out in the barn. Plum Puddin', Purple Mouse and Todd look at each other and then start running out the door to go see what's the matter. As they get to the barn door, they hear a loud kicking on it. Plum opens it and there stands Todd's horse Glister hollering, "Charcoal is starting to foal!"

Plum Puddin', Purple Mouse and Todd look at each other shocked that Glister can talk, and Plum Puddin says, "Glister, we had no idea you could talk!"

To which Glister raises a hoof and says, "Surprise!"

They all crack up laughing and Todd looks at Glister and says, "Glister, you mean you have been able to talk all these years?"

Glister grins and whinnies and then answers, "Yes, I have been able too. I'm sorry I didn't tell you, but I figured I would learn more if I kept my mouth shut," and then they all laugh again.

Plum Puddin' looks at Todd and says, "You really didn't know this, did you?"

Todd gets a big grin on his face and shaking his head, he jokingly says, "Neigh!"

That causes all of them to break out in laughter again and then Plum Puddin' says, "Wonders never cease! Well, let's go over to the stall and see what Charcoal is giving birth to."

So, Glister, Plum Puddin', Purple Mouse and Todd rush to the stall to find Charcoal giving birth to the new foal-a baby boy horse. After he is born, Charcoal and Brownback lovingly look at each other and then at their new one and Charcoal asks Brownback, "What should we name him?"

Brownback answers, "I don't care. The main thing is that he's healthy and he's our own! Our very special gift from God!"

When Brownback said, "The Main Thing," it triggered a thought in Charcoals mind. "How about Mane?" she asks.

"Yes, that's perfect. Let's call him that!" answers Brownback.

"So, Mane it is," says Charcoal. They look up and by now the rest of the gang has come to the barn to see the new arrival.

"Oh, isn't she beautiful," says Dosi Doe.

"Yes, but she is a he," says Plum Puddin'.

Dosi Doe laughs and says, "Oops" and then says, "Congratulations Charcoal and Brownback, I'm happy for you. My name is Dosi Doe and the gang picked me up yesterday because I was lost."

"It's nice to meet you Dosi Doe," they both say.

Then Dosi Doe looks at Mane and says, "Welcome to the world little one," and everyone joins in giving Brownback and Charcoal words of Congratulations

7 - BRANSON BOUND

Today has sure started off with a lot of excitement," says Plum Puddin's friend Gaylene.

"Yeah, it sure has and there's more excitement to come, 'cause now we gotta work on plans on how to surprise Branson The Balladeer once we get Dosi Doe to the North Pole," says Plum Puddin'.

Dosi Doe's eyes light up and she asks, "Before we go up to the North Pole, could we please go to Branson to let Mama and Daddy know I am safe and that Branson The Balladeer is alive?"

Plum Puddin' answers, "Yes, that's a great idea Dosi Doe and we would be happy to do that for you. But first, I'd like to go by Knob Lick and pick up my Daddy Darrell and my Mama Rose Marie so they can meet you and go with us on our trip."

"Oh yes, I would love to meet your parents Plum Puddin'," says Dosi Doe.

Then Plum Puddin' asks Todd, "Can we use you and Glister and your wagon to take us to Branson please?"

Todd replies, "Yes, I would be more than happy to take you all. I never pass up an opportunity to go to Branson!"

So, Plum Puddin' and Todd go to his cabin and pick up Todd's wagon and then come back and gather up the gang and off they go to Knob Lick to pick up his Daddy Darrell and his Mama Rose Marie at their cabin.

8 - SNOWCAP

As they go through the forest toward Knob Lick, they start smelling something awful. Everyone in the wagon suddenly realizes what it is and they start groaning and holding their noses. Pinecone starts barking and then buries his head in Plum Puddin's side. Plum Puddin' says, "Todd, please go faster. We gotta get away from that smell!" Plum Puddin' looks over at Purple Mouse and he's a bright purple! Plum Puddin' says to him, "Purple Mouse, you're as purple as a grape! Did you know that you would turn that color when you smelled something really strong?"

Purple Mouse answers, "No, I never knew I could do that, but as bad as it is, it's a wonder I don't turn white and pass out!" and then he laughs.

"No, white is my color Purple Mouse," jokes Snowdeer.

"And I'm about to turn green," Maroon Mouse says. Orchid can't say anything as she laughs and gasps for air!

The smell gets worse and worse and Todd speeds up, but he finally realizes the only way that would make it better is to turn around and go back. Just as Todd is about to turn around, Terrie Young Deer says, "Wait! I see something in the path ahead!" As they look forward, about 20 feet in front of them, they see a skunk walking across the path! The skunk, thinking he is being moved in on, gets ready to spray the gang.

But Plum Puddin' sees what's happening, raises his hands and says, "Please, Mr. Skunk, don't spray us! We don't mean you any harm!"

The skunk stops right in his tracks and asks, "Who are you?"

Then the whole gang introduces themselves and the skunk quickly changes his attitude! He begins to smile and says, "Hello, my name is Snowcap. What brings you to this part of the forest?"

Plum Puddin' says, "We're headed to Knob Lick to see my Daddy Darrell and my Mama Rose Marie."

"That's great you have family who live so close," says Snowcap.

"Yes, I am very thankful for them and I am also thankful for my family here in this wagon. They may not be blood kin, but they are family, just the same." says Plum Puddin'.

"Where are you from Snowcap?" asks Purple Mouse.

Snowcap gets a sad look on his face and says, "I'm from Skunk Holler Forest, over by Branson. I somehow got separated from my family while we were roaming around this area. Then the big snowstorm came and caused me to lose sight of them. The reason we were out was because we were looking for our friend, Branson The Balladeer who, a long time ago was coming to go Christmas Caroling with me and my family. He got lost in a snowstorm and we never did find him. Even though he's been missing for so long, we still go out and try to see if we can find him. That is what we were doing when this last snowstorm came. I lost track of my family and even though I set off my smell during the storm, they didn't smell my scent. I love them and I'm trying to find my way back."

Plum Puddin', Purple Mouse, Snowdeer and Dosi Doe look at each other and start to smile. Then Dosi Due says, "Snowcap, you may not believe this, but I am Branson The Balladeer's sister Dosi Doe! I am so honored that you have been looking for my brother! Thank you! I also had been out looking for Branson, but I got lost in the snowstorm and Snowdeer, Plum Puddin' and the gang found me! And now we have found you! Snowcap, you don't have to search for Branson The Balladeer anymore because I found out he lives at the North Pole with Santa! And not only that, Snowdeer, Plum Puddin' and Purple Mouse go to see him up there!"

Snowcap looks at her in amazement and doesn't believe what he is hearing. Plum Puddin' sees his unbelief and he asks, "Snowcap, would you like to go with us? After we pick up my Daddy Darrell and my Mama Rose Marie, we're headin' for Branson to let Dosi Doe's parents know that she is alright and that Branson The Balladeer is alive and well and is living up at the North Pole with Santa! If you would come with us Snowcap, we will take you to the North Pole and you can see him for yourself! Want to come?"

Snowcap now believes it and he says, "Oh definitely yes! I want to see my friend again and I want to go back to Branson." So, Snowcap joins the gang on the wagon and they head toward Knob Lick. While they are on their way, Dosi Doe asks, "How did you get to know my brother Branson?"

Snowcap replies, "I am a big lover of music and your brother would always come to Skunk Holler Forest during the Christmas and Easter Seasons to sing and play! He would sing many of the songs he wrote himself and he would sing to anybody and everybody! Branson never met a stranger."

"We are definitely talking about the same deer," laughs Dosi Doe.

Snowcap then says, "Sometime, I want you all to come to Skunk Holler Forest and meet my family and friends! We're always singing and playing music and pulling pranks on each other!"

"It sounds like you can be quite a "STINKER" Snowcap," jokes Purple Mouse.

They all laugh and Snowcap acts like he is going to spray him, but then stops and laughs and says, "Yes, I can be. You never know when I will cause a stink!" This causes them to bust out in laughter and they can tell they have made a great new friend.

"Hey look! There's Knob Lick ahead," says Todd, and they go a little way farther and stop in front of Daddy Darrell and Mama Rose Marie's cabin. Plum

Puddin' and Pinecone jump off the wagon and go to the door and knock. Darrell answers the door and hugs his son and pets Pinecone's head. Rose Marie is right behind him, and she looks at Plum Puddin' with a surprised look as she wonders why they would be there at this time of day. But, she hugs him and Pinecone and then looks at the loaded wagon and waves. Darrell also waves at the gang and then asks, "What are y'all doing here Son?"

Plum Puddin' answers, "Mama-Daddy! I have so much to tell you! But first, would you like to go on a trip to Branson? I'll tell you what's going on while we're on our way!"

"Yes, we would love to go with you," they both reply and they gather their coats and get on the wagon. After they take off, Plum Puddin' tells them about Brownback and Charcoal having a new foal and that they named him Mane. Then, he introduces Dosi Doe to them and tells them she is Branson The Balladeer's sister and that their family lives in Branson. He goes on to tell them about her getting lost and how they found her in the forest. And next, Plum introduces his folks to Snowcap and tells them he's a friend of Branson The Balladeer too.

Darrell and Rose Marie smile at both of them and tell them what a pleasure it is to meet them. Then, Darrell says to Dosi Doe, "Your brother has meant a lot to Plum Puddin' and to us and all the gang, and we are really happy you are going to the North Pole to see him."

Rose Marie looks at Dosi Doe and says, "When we were up at the North Pole, we all fell in love with Branson, and we loved to hear him play and sing. Now, we look forward to knowing you and going to your country community of Branson with you and meeting your family. We all love how your parents named your brother Branson after the community."

Dosi Doe answers, "Thank you all very much. It has been an honor to meet you all and the rest of the gang and I look forward to knowing everyone here a lot better and spending a lot of time together." Everyone smiles and Pinecone goes over to Dosi Doe and puts his head against her leg and gives a contented whimper.

Todd is so excited to get to Branson and see the great reunion between Dosi Doe and her parents, so he makes a clicking sound with his mouth and tells Glister to giddy up so they can get there sooner. Glister instantly picks up the speed and away they go!

9 - THE HAMPTONS & THE COUNTS

As they make their way to Branson, the sun shines bright and the weather warms up, making the snow melt. Dosi Doe, Plum Puddin' and Todd Lott are up in the front of the wagon and get to talking about Branson and Todd says, "I've been to Branson more times than I can remember. I enjoy fishin' in the White River and at Bull Creek and listening to the old time fiddle, banjo, wash tub, doghouse bass and all the singers singin'. I take my family there whenever I get a chance. I know the Branson area of the Ozarks like the back of my hand."

Then Dosi Doe says, "I love it too and I miss it so much and I look forward to getting back and seeing my family before we go to the North Pole. I'm excited to introduce you all to my family. They will really appreciate what you all have done for me and for my brother."

"We look forward to meeting your family Dosi Doe," says Plum Puddin'.

Then all of a sudden, Todd turns around in the wagon seat and raises his voice and says to everyone, "I've got some friends coming up over at Gumbo Mountain that I want you to meet. They're my friends, the Hamptons and the Counts. I always go visit them when I'm on my trips to Branson."

After hearing their names, Plum Puddin' lights up and says, "Yea, we know them too! Let's go pay 'em a visit."

So, in a little bit, they come to Gumbo Mountain and sitting on it is a bunch of log cabins with large plots of dirt in the back where they raise big gardens. There are trees with clothes hanging on clothes lines strung from one tree to another. The Gumbo Log Cabin Church is sitting higher up on the hill with its hand carved doors and big church bell right above them. When Todd says whoa to Glister, folks hear him and they start coming out of the log cabins and the church.

"Hey Todd, how you doing?" asks a friendly hill man.

"Doin' fine Counts," Todd replies.

Then the man looks over the whole group and says, "Well, I'll be, there's Darrell and Rose Marie! How are you all?"

Darrell and Rose Marie smile at their longtime friend Counts and they put out their hands to shake his hand. Darrell says, "We're doing just fine Counts. Great to see you! How's Barbara and the rest of the family? And where's Hampton?"

Counts replies, "He's over in his cabin with Brenda and the family workin' on his comedy act where he plays the character, "Nearly Famous." He's really funny and I keep tellin' him one day he'll have to travel all over the country and make people laugh!"

Rose Marie laughs and says, "Have him and the family come over and I'll make them some chicken and dumplings and we'll put together our own show! And you all are invited too!"

Counts says, "We'll have to take you up on that." Then Counts looks at Plum Puddin' and he says, "Plum Puddin', how are you doing?"

"Doin' great Mr. Counts," Plum replies. Some of the gang in the wagon look at each other puzzled as to why they would refer to some of the family with only their last names. Darrell notices their confused looks and he says, "The reason we say their last names so much is because almost everyone here at Gumbo Mountain has the last name of Hampton or Counts and there's so many of them, we mostly just call them by their last name 'cause we can't remember them all!" Everyone laughs and while they are laughing, they see Hampton, Brenda, Barbara and the family walking down the mountain. When they reach the gang, they all speak and Hampton says, "I heard some laughing and I had to see where it was coming from. I thought I'd come down and tell some jokes 'cause you were already in a laughing mood and I would have a ready-made audience!" Everyone laughs again and then Hampton sees his friends Darrell, Rose Marie and Plum Puddin' and he asks, "What are you all doing in these parts?"

Darrell says, "Headin' over to Branson. We have a little doe here who's looking for her family who lives over there." Then Darrell tells Dosi Doe's story to the Counts and the Hamptons.

When he is finished, Barbara says, "What a story Dosi Doe! We will be praying for you,"

Brenda says, "Dosi Doe, we have met your brother Branson The Balladeer many times. He has sang in our church here on Gumbo Mountain where I lead the music and he has sang some songs there with our daughter Lauren."

Dosi Doe smiles and says, "Thank you for your prayers Barbara. And thank you Brenda for telling me about my brother singing in your church. We never knew how far away he would go to sing."

Then Lauren says, "Would you introduce us to your friends please? We'd love to meet them."

"Sure, I'd be happy to," says Darrell, so, he makes his round introducing all the gang on the wagon to them. Then, the Hamptons and the Counts, being the friendly folks they are, introduce themselves, using both their first and last names!

Then Counts asks, "Want to stay for supper and spend the night and head out to Branson in the morning? Barb and Brenda and the girls will fix you something to eat."

Darrell says, "Thank you, but we need to keep moving on towards Branson 'cause this little deer is anxious to get home. But, all of us do wanna come back and we'll take you up on that meal offer. And we want to go to church too." Then Darrell looks at the gang and says, "Counts is the preacher here at the Church on Gumbo

Mountain. He has led a many a soul to the Lord here and has dunked a many a person in baptism over in the St. Francis River, so we'd better be good around him!"

Everyone laughs and Counts laughs and says, "I love working for the Lord and I love my family and my friends and you all are welcome any time."

Darrell, Rose Marie, Plum Puddin', Snowdeer and the gang thank them and tell them goodbye.

Hampton and the rest tell them goodbye and Counts says, "God bless and have a safe trip and come back to see us soon."

So, off the Plum Puddin' gang go, with warm hearts from visiting with great friends and excitement growing as they get closer to Branson.

10 - REUBEN AND MARY

A few hours later, the gang pulls up in front of a post office with several log cabins and a lake flowing in the distance. "Well, here we are. We're at Branson," says Todd to the wagon load of friends.

Plum Puddin' looks up at the post office sign that says, "BRANSON" and with a big grin he says, "Dosi Doe-you're home! As he says this, he looks around for Dosi Doe, but she has already jumped off the wagon and is headed to the post office porch.

All of a sudden, a man with a beard and mustache comes to the door and as he's beginning to ask, "Can I help Y'all?" he sees Dosi Doe running toward him.

"Daddy!" exclaims Dosi Doe.

"My little Dosi Doe!" the excited gentleman says as he runs to her. He picks her up in his arms and swirls her around and says, "We've missed you so much! What happened to you? We thought maybe you were..."

Dosi Doe interrupts him and says, "I'm so sorry Daddy. I got lost in a snowstorm just like Branson did, but Snowdeer, Plum Puddin' and Purple Mouse found me."

"Oh, thank you all very much for bringing my little girl back to me," says the kind man.

Snowdeer, Plum Puddin' and Purple Mouse don't know what to say or to think because Dosi Doe calls this human her daddy!

Dosi Doe and her daddy see their faces and realize they didn't know he would be human and so the man says, "Let me clear this up. My name is Reuben Branson. Once upon a time, me and my wife Mary found Dosi Doe and her brother Branson in these hills by Lake Taneycomo. The lake you see over there." He points over to the beautiful flowing river, just down the hill and then he continues, "Their parents were gone and we never did find out what happened to them, so Mary and I took them in and raised them as our own." Reuben then turns around and opens the front door and hollers, "Mary! Please come out here! Got somethin' to show you!"

They see a woman peek through one of the post office windows and then they hear her voice loudly saying, "Dosi Doe! My Dosi Doe is back!" Then she runs out of the cabin to the porch and kneels in front of Dosi Doe and throws her arms around her and gives her a big hug. Then she asks, "Dosi Doe, what happened to you my dear?"

Dosi Doe answers, "Mama, I got lost in the winter storm and couldn't find my way back."

With tears in her eyes, Mary says, "O, how we both missed you! We lost your brother Branson and we couldn't bear to lose you too!"

Then Dosi Doe says, "Daddy, Mama, I have some wonderful news to tell you. Branson the Balladeer is alive! He got lost in these mountains in a snowstorm and didn't know where he was. Then Santa found him and took him to the North Pole."

Reuben and Mary's mouths drop open and Reuben asks, "How can that be? How could you know Santa found our Branson The Balladeer?"

Dosi Doe replies, "Plum Puddin', Snowdeer, and Purple Mouse have been to the North Pole because Santa has given each of them a magical jar that takes them there. They have seen Branson The Balladeer themselves and now they have offered to take me there to surprise him!"

Reuben and Mary can hardly believe they are hearing right, but they want to hear more and they excitedly ask Plum Puddin', Snowdeer and the gang to come with them to their home.

Dosi Doe breaks in and says, "Before we go inside, please let me introduce you to the gang Mama and Daddy," so Dosi Doe introduces everyone to Reuben and Mary.

After they have met them all, Reuben says, "Mary, would you please fix our guests some supper and I'll close up the post office for the night and then I'll meet you at the cabin."

Mary excitedly replies, "Yes! I would love to! Come on over and wash up and I'll get supper going."

So, they all go over to Reuben and Mary Branson's cabin, except for Plum Puddin', Snowdeer and Purple Mouse who want to stay with Reuben while he locks up. After they get inside the post office, Plum Puddin', Snowdeer and Purple Mouse look around and then Plum Puddin' asks Reuben, "How long have you been here sir?"

Reuben answers, "A long, long time Plum Puddin'. Since my last name is Branson, I decided to name this little area of the country after myself and my wife because we love the Ozarks so much. I just felt the good Lord wanted me to name it that and so I did!"

Then Snowdeer says, "Mr. Branson, you have done so much for the Ozarks and for Dosi Doe and Branson the Balladeer. We are sure honored to meet you and Mrs. Branson."

Purple Mouse then says, "None of us ever knew why it was called Branson or how Branson the Balladeer got his name. We are really happy to know now how it came to be."

Reuben says, "I'll tell you how Branson The Balladeer got his name. When the Mrs. and I found him at a young age, he was hummin' and trying to sing. Can you imagine how shocked we were to find out he could talk? Ha ha!" laughs Reuben.

21

"They took a likin' to us and we loved them as our own. Our cabin was always filled with music and we loved that."

Then Plum Puddin' says, "That's wonderful and I have to tell you that he's still singing and writing! At the North Pole he sings to all the elves and everyone up there, even Santa and Mrs. Santa!"

"O, how I want to see him and hear him sing again," says Reuben.

"O, you will, if we have anything to do with it," says Plum Puddin'. Then Reuben says, "Well, my friends, I'm gonna lock up and let's get over to the cabin. Miss Mary will be having a big feast for you all if I know her, and I know her!" he laughs.

As they all sit down to supper, Reuben gives the Thanks for the food and then Mary says to dig in. Reuben is curious about Plum Puddin' and his friends being able to go to the North Pole, so he asks Plum Puddin', "Why were you given a magical jar that made it where you could go visit Santa?"

Plum Puddin' points to his parents and replies, "I grew up eating Plum Pudding that my mama Rose Marie made me. Because I loved it so much, my daddy Darrell and mama Rose Marie nick-named me Plum Puddin'. My real name is Randy, but Plum Puddin' just kinda stuck." Then he laughs.

"How interesting. I love Plum Pudding too. It's my favorite," says Reuben.

Plum Puddin' gets a big grin on his face and continues, "I gave Santa a big jar of Plum Pudding one year for Christmas and to say thank you, Santa gave me a magical jar. In the jar was a note that said whenever I wanted to go to the North Pole, all I had to do was hold that magical jar in my right hand and say the magic words, "HO-HO-HO! Off TO THE NORTH POLE WE GO!" and Santa's magical Sugar Snow would come and whisk me and Pinecone away to see Santa, Mrs. Santa, the Elves, The Mew Family, Strike The Bell, and so many others...AND your Son, Branson The Balladeer."

"What an amazing story, says Reuben. I used to teach school before I settled down here and opened the post office. How I wish I had known this story back then, 'cause I would of told it to all of the children! Mary and I are so blessed to have met you all and we appreciate how you're helpin' us."

Then Plum Puddin' says, "Thank You, Mr. Branson, that is nice of you to say. I can promise you that you'll have even more stories to tell once we get back from taking Dosi Doe to the North Pole to be reunited with Branson The Balladeer."

"Yes, that's for sure and you can bet I'll be tellin' every one of 'em," says Reuben laughing. Then he turns to Snowdeer and Purple Mouse and asks, "Will You please tell us your stories of how you got your magical jars and what happened on your visit with Santa?"

So, they both happily do so and the stories go well into the night. Mary says, "Even though we just met, I feel we're more like family."

"Yes, Mam, I feel that way too," replies Rose Marie.

"Well, it looks like our family has gotten even bigger on this trip," laughs Darrell. As the stories continue, the food also continues to be eaten, 'till only empty dishes remain on the table.

Later that night, Mary says to Reuben, "Let's have them all stay the night so they can get rested up before they head back to Knob Lick."

"Yes, dear, that's a wonderful idea," answers Reuben.

There's so many of them in the group that there aren't enough beds, so Mary and Reuben tell them they'll make pallets on the floor. But, before any pallets have been made, Reuben and Mary start sharing stories about how they came to settle in the Branson area and so, more stories began. Everyone is so excited to have met this wonderful couple and to hear their stories, that no one wants to go to bed.

Once everyone has finally gone to bed, Darrell whispers to Rose Marie, "I'm sure glad the Branson's came here and named this part of the country after themselves. Their southern hospitality makes them the perfect people to have a community named after."

The next morning, by the time everyone had awoken, Reuben had already started his day over at the post office and Mary was already up and fixing breakfast. The smell of the homemade biscuits baking at the fireplace makes them perk up and flock to the table. Rose Marie helps Mary set the table and then notices Mary going to the cupboard and bringing out jars of Plum Pudding. They both laugh as Mary puts them on the table. When Plum Puddin' sees the jars, he gives a holler and all of them start laughing at him. Mary says, "Plum Puddin', I'm gonna take up the biscuits now. Would You please run some of them over to Reuben along with his sausage, eggs and Plum Pudding?"

"Yes Ma'am, I'd be happy to," replies Plum Puddin'. Then he gets to thinking he would love to eat with Reuben and he asks, "Can I take my meal over and eat with him please?"

"Why yes my dear, you are more than welcome to. Reuben would love your company, but, I'll warn you. He might put you to work!" says Mary laughing.

"That'll be the day when Plum Puddin' works," jokes Snowdeer. Plum Puddin' blushes and everyone laughs. Snowdeer says, "Hey Plum, I thought Purple Mouse was the only one who blushed!" At that saying, Plum Puddin' blushes even more and Purple Mouse joins in blushing his purple color.

Then Plum Puddin' says, "Alright, I'm gonna get out of here. I've had enough abuse for one day." Then he laughs and out the cabin door he goes with two big plates of biscuits, sausages, eggs and Plum Pudding followed by a purple faced Purple Mouse carrying his big plate of breakfast.

After breakfast, Snowdeer, Plum Puddin' and Purple Mouse go out into the forest with the gang. As they near the lake, their friend Taneycomo says, "This is the lake I was named after. I don't get here as often as I would like, but when I do, I stay for hours and fish, canoe and walk the mountains."

Terrie Young Deer says, "I love it here! What a beautiful place! I want to canoe here sometime."

"Ok, we will do that," answers Taneycomo. Then he looks up the river and says, "Over there a little way off of Lake Taneycomo is Turkey Creek. Wanna go see it?" They all say yes and off they go walking the shoreline of Lake Taneycomo to where Turkey Creek comes in.

"It's nice and peaceful and you can see some folks fishin' from time to time," says Taneycomo.

But, before they come to Turkey Creek, Snowdeer sees some familiar deer and with a surprised voice he says, "Mama! Daddy! Uncle Ken-Buck! What are you all doin' here?"

"We're just here visiting Branson along with your Uncle Ken-Buck," replies Deerlores who is Snowdeer's mama. Then Jim-Buck, Snowdeer's daddy says, "Your Uncle Ken-Buck is showing us around and told us that Branson is a great place to visit and we agree with him!"

"I've been comin' here for years Snowdeer, says Ken-Buck. It just seems the good Lord put an invisible magnet in these parts, drawing all kinds of animals to come here. And humans too! A lot of them have moved here and are callin' it home."

"I love it here too, says Snowdeer. The Ozark Mountains are my favorite and If I lived anywhere else besides Doe Run, it would be either up at the North Pole with Santa or right here in Branson!"

"If you moved to the North Pole, Purple Mouse could come visit you up there and use that as an excuse to see Tasha Mouse," jokes Plum Puddin'. When he says that, everyone looks at Purple Mouse who has by now blushed his purple color again.

They all laugh and Deerlores asks, "Snowdeer, when are you gonna go back to pay Santa a visit?"

Snowdeer replies, "Real soon Mama." Then Snowdeer starts telling Deerlores, Jim-Buck and Ken-Buck the story about Dosi Doe, Branson The Balladeer and meeting Reuben and Mary Branson. They say they want to meet them too and so Plum Puddin', Snowdeer and Purple Mouse take Snowdeer's folks over to meet Reuben and Mary.

The Branson's treat Snowdeer's mama, daddy and uncle with the same hospitality as they treated him. Jim-Buck says, "Mr. and Mrs. Branson, we will for sure be back to see your beautiful community. Thank you for all you both have done."

"My friend, you are just seeing the beginning of many things to come," replies Reuben.

Then Ken-Buck says, "Mr. and Mrs. Branson, I will be back too and I look forward to visiting with you whenever I'm here."

"I'll look forward to it Ken-Buck," says Reuben. Then Mary says, "When you all come back, I'll fix a meal for all of You."

"Thank You, Mrs. Branson," says Deerlores.

Dosi Doe looks at her father and asks, "Daddy, would you go back to Knob Lick with us and then go to the North Pole?"

Reuben answers, "My daughter, I would love to go with you, but I have to stay and watch the post office and the town." Then Reuben looks at Plum Puddin' and says, "I do want to go with you to the North Pole someday. Could the Mrs. and I do that sometime later?"

"Yes, Sir, you are welcome to go anytime," answers Plum Puddin'.

"Wonderful! Then I will stay here and you all head out for Knob Lick and I will talk with You soon. Or, you can send me a letter. I'll be the first one to see it," says Reuben laughing.

They all laugh at that and Plum Puddin' says, "I don't write letters much, but I will be back to visit with you soon! Thank you for everything, Mr. and Mrs. Branson." Then he turns to the gang and says, "Well, we better get going."

Todd says, "Ok, let's load the wagon and I'll count to make sure everyone is on."

As they load up, Mary runs to the cabin and returns with a picnic basket. She lifts the cover and shows them extra jars of Plum Pudding and biscuits. Then she says, "Here's some more biscuits and Plum Pudding to eat on your way to Knob Lick so you won't go hungry." Then she looks at Plum Puddin' and gets a grin on her face and says to him, "Now don't you go eatin' all of it. Save some for the rest of the gang!" Everyone laughs and after Todd has counted everybody present on the wagon, they begin to say their goodbyes.

But before Todd tells Glister to go, Jim-Buck, Deerlores and Ken-Buck ask if they can go back with them to Knob Lick. Snowdeer says, "Yes, you all can go, but then he gets an ornery grin on his face and looks at his Uncle Ken-Buck and says, "You have to promise me you'll make me a special batch of PineCone Chips though!"

"Ok, I promise Snowdeer," says Ken-Buck laughing. So, Jim-Buck, Deerlores and Ken-Buck jump on the wagon and everyone waves goodbye and off they head back to Knob Lick.

11 - CARROT THE RABBIT

As the gang leave Reuben and Mary Branson's cabin, they take one more look at Lake Taneycomo. Their Indian friend Taneycomo, who was named after the lake says, "I take great pride in being named after this lake. The name Taneycomo is taken from Taney County Missouri and many of my ancestors have crossed it to explore the Ozark Mountains and to go fishing, bear hunting and cow tipping."

"Cow tipping?" asks Dosi Doe.

"Yes, cow tipping," answers Taneycomo. "Our Tribe of Cherokee would leave our tepees late at night and go over to Garber and sneak up on some of the cattle and catch them while they were sleeping on all four legs and then push them over."

"Really?" asks Dosi Doe.

"Yea," answered Taneycomo.

Plum Puddin' adds to the conversation and says, "O yes, I have done that many times over in Possum Holler."

"I've helped you do that a few times too," says Snowdeer.

"And I have done that too," adds Purple Mouse.

"I don't believe any of you," says Dosi Doe and Taneycomo, Plum Puddin', Snowdeer and Purple Mouse just laugh.

"Have y'all ever seen the Spook Light?" Plum Puddin' asks.

"Yes, I have, answers Ken-Buck. Your Daddy Jim-Buck and me used to go in the woods over by Springfield and see it."

Then Jim-Buck says, "One time when we were there, the Spook Light started floatin' really really fast through the woods toward us and we tore out of there like mad men, or should I say, 'Mad Deer', and then he and Ken-Buck laugh.

"But, we went back there a lot of times after that and saw the light every time," said Ken-Buck.

"Wanna go there sometime Snowdeer?" asks Jim-Buck.

"We already did....oops...." Plum Puddin' blurts out and then he stops talking 'cause he realized he told something that was a secret between him and his two friends. Jim-Buck and Deerlores look at Snowdeer and Darrell and Rose Marie look at Plum Puddin'. Then Purple Mouse's Mom Orchid and his Dad Maroon look at him waiting to see if he was guilty too.

Purple Mouse looks down and says, "Ok, I confess, Snowdeer, Plum Puddin' and I took a trip..."

"You mean that trip where you were gone all night and had us all worried sick?" asks Orchid.

Purple Mouse blushes a bright purple and says, "Yes mam, that's the time."

Then Orchid breaks out in a grin and says, "That's ok, you made it home safe, but if you ever go again, you better ask us to go too!" Then she laughs and that makes everyone else laugh.

Then Darrell says, "Yes, Orchid is right. If you go again, we're all going, We're not gonna miss out on a great time!" and then he laughs. The parents get a kick out of seeing their children feel like they were gonna get in bad trouble.

In a little bit, they come up to the tiny country community of Garber. They see a few cabins and an old church with a big cross on top and clothes hanging on clotheslines like they all do in the hills. "Reminds me of Knob Lick," says Rose Marie and Orchid and Deerlores nod in agreement.

"Hey, there's a mountain stream. Let's stop and get some water," says Jim-Buck.

"Ok, I'm sure Glister could use a drink," answers Todd. So everyone gets off the wagon and heads to the creek. "This is Roark Creek," says Todd. Joel Garber lives here and is a preacher and a spokesman for this community."

"How'd you know that?" asks Snowdeer.

"My friend John Fullerton who is a historian and singer in these parts told me," answers Todd.

As they are all drinking from Roark Creek, they hear a voice deep in the woods. "Wanna go see what it is?" asks Plum Puddin'.

"You bet!" answers Snowdeer and Purple Mouse.

So, the three of them start their venture over some hills and then down in a holler they come up on a big rabbit den, nestled between a fallen tree and Roark Creek. As they slowly walk up to a tiny window that's open, they hear someone talking loud to himself. When they peek in, their jaws drop as they see a rabbit standing there with a Christmas tree fully lit with candles and beautiful Christmas decorations all over half of the den. The other half is all decorated with an Easter tree with candles glowing on it and beautiful pastel colored eggs hanging on it. Easter baskets filled with Pinecone Chips, candies and chocolate Easter bunnies are all over the place. Hanging on the walls are picture after picture of his rabbit family.

"Why don't they accept me like I am!" the rabbit complains over and over out loud to himself. Purple Mouse sneezes outside the window and the rabbit hears it and gasps and hops in surprise. Purple Mouse turns purple when he realizes what he has done. All three of them look at each other and quickly bend down below the window so the rabbit won't see them. The rabbit hops over to the door and opens it a little bit to see who it is. When he sees them, he asks very timidly, "Who are you?" But before they can answer, the rabbit looks right at Snowdeer and says, "My! How rare to see a deer such as yourself!"

Snowdeer answers, "Yes, I know. I'm the only deer I've ever seen that is solid white! Oh, please let me introduce myself. My name is Snowdeer and these are my friends, Plum Puddin' and Purple Mouse."

The rabbit quickly stops being nervous and they see a smile break upon his face. Then he says, "Hello, my name is Carrot. Once upon a time, Daddy Rabbit, Mama Rabbit and myself were passing through here at Garber and we liked it and decided to stay a while. Then, soon came along all my brothers and sisters, and I mean ALL my brothers and sisters, and we decided to make this our home. We soon became friends with Joel Garber-the man who named this part of the woods after himself. We would get together and have square dances and pie suppers and cake walks and even to this day we do things together. He and his family live on the other side of Roark Creek."

Snowdeer enjoys Carrot's story, but he has to know why Carrot was talking to himself like he was when they came up to his den. So he asks, "Carrot, why were you so upset with yourself? We heard you a half a mile away from your den."

Carrot replies, "It's because they won't accept me. None of my family will accept me for liking Christmas just as much as Easter."

"O, don't worry about that Carrot," says Snowdeer. Then he looks at Plum Puddin' and Purple Mouse and they also tell him not to worry about that. Then, Snowdeer looks at Carrot and says, "Christmas is our favorite time of year. But many love Easter just as much as Christmas. There are some who like it even more." Plum Puddin' and Purple Mouse both nod in agreement and Snowdeer continues, "Besides, both seasons are very important. At Christmas, we celebrate God's Son Jesus, who was born in a stable in Bethlehem to Mary and Joseph. Then at Easter, we celebrate that same person, Jesus, who by now was grown and in his thirties. He was put to death on a cross at Jerusalem and died for all men, so that whoever puts their trust in Him would go to Heaven when they died."

"So, that's what pastor Joel Garber was talking about," says Carrot.

Snowdeer answers, "Yes, it sure is and that is the main thing to always remember about Easter. But, there's also the fun side of Easter, with chocolate bunnies, candies and Easter Egg hunts with families all over the world. There's also the fun side of Christmas that has celebrations all around the world with presents and Santa Claus and lots of food!" he says and laughs.

Carrot smiles and says, "Thank you for explaining this to me. I see it all so much clearer now and I believe all that you said."

"That's great, says Snowdeer, but would you want to hear something you might have trouble believing?"

"Yes, please tell me," answers Carrot. Then Snowdeer goes into his story about his wish to go to the North Pole to pull Santa's sleigh and deliver presents to all the good children and animals in the world. He tells Carrot how his wish was granted by Santa and how Santa gave him a magical jar that would take him to the North Pole and how he can still go there-even if it isn't Christmas.

Carrot stands there amazed and says, "Next time you go to the North Pole, can I go too please?"

They all laugh and Plum Puddin' says, "Yes, you sure can. We have a lot more to tell you Carrot and your life will never be the same!" They laugh again and Plum Puddin' continues, "Come to Possum Holler with us. We have a wagon full of friends waiting for us right now and we're plannin' on going to the North Pole again in a day or two!"

Carrot hops up and down and says, "Ok, I'll go blow out the candles on the trees and grab a coat and we'll be on our way!"

Snowdeer, Plum Puddin' and Purple Mouse stand just outside Carrot's door and look in and watch him hop from one tree to the other blowing out the candles. As they look around, they are fascinated at all the decorations he has and the many pictures framed on his wall of family members. As Carrot hops out the door to leave with his new friends, he smiles a big smile and they make their way to the wagon and Plum Puddin' introduces them all.

As they are riding on the way over to Possum Holler, Snowdeer, Plum Puddin' and Purple Mouse spend that time telling Carrot about their families and how they became friends and how they can get to the North Pole using the magical jars Santa gave them. They fill him in on many of the people at the North Pole and tell him how they're going to have Dosi Doe meet up and surprise her brother Branson The Balladeer, who doesn't know she's coming. By the time they arrive at Plum Puddin's cabin, Carrot-who has a great memory-is prepared and ready to go to the North Pole.

12 - DOSI DOE AND THE NORTH POLE

By the time they reach Possum Holler and Plum Puddin's cabin, they're all so tired that Plum asks if they would like to stay the night. They accept his offer, and the next morning when they all wake up, Plum Puddin' is already making breakfast and had already fed the animals and gathered the eggs. They have a great country breakfast and Plum says to Dosi Doe, "Are you ready to go to the North Pole today?"

"O Yes!" she replies.

Everyone else says they are ready to go too and Plum Puddin' laughs and says, "The North Pole ain't gonna know what hit 'em when we arrive!" They all laugh and Plum Puddin' asks Snowdeer and Purple Mouse to go to the cupboard and get their magical jars. When they return with them, Plum Puddin' says, "Let's gather by the fireplace and everyone say the magic words, "HO-HO-HO! OFF TO THE NORTH POLE WE GO" at the same time, Ok?" Everyone excitedly says, "OK" and so they gather around the fireplace and Plum Puddin' says he'll count it off and for them to start saying the magic words on the count of 3. Plum Puddin', Snowdeer and Purple Mouse hold their magical jars in their right hand and Plum Puddin' says, "Ok, let's go! 1-2-3......."HO-HO-HO! OFF TO THE NORTH POLE WE GO!!!" They close their eyes thinking this is it, but nothing happens.

Dosi Doe looks down and says, "Oh No! I should of known it wouldn't work for me. Now I'll never see Branson The Balladeer!" Then, all of a sudden in the distance, they hear Santa laughing! They look at each other in amazement and then see Sugar Snow magic dust coming through Plum Puddin's fireplace and swirl around them! They gasp and then laugh and in an instant-they're gone!

Next thing they know, they're flying through the air, circled with Sugar Snow magic dust and heading straight to Santa and The North Pole! As the Sugar Snow lowers them at the North Pole's Pole, they look at the beautiful sight of this snowy Christmas Kingdom. Snowdeer, Plum Puddin' and Purple Mouse hold tightly on to their bright and beaming magical jars and gaze in child-like wonder at their surroundings. They all watch as elves and their families teeter totter together while others slide down miles and miles of different colored slides. Other elves, along with other villagers, are gathered around visiting and eating snow cones covered with different colored toppings. The crisp clear Christmas sounds of Holiday music are coming out of giant speakers from the North Pole's own Christmas station, CMAS. Snowdeer, Plum Puddin' and the gang start getting into the music and dancing around and Pinecone-Plum Puddin's pet dog, starts barking and rolling in the snow.

All of a sudden, running up to them comes the official voice of CMAS-the North Pole's own JB the DJ Elf, who's holding a microphone and wanting to do a radio interview with them. He says, "Welcome Snowdeer, Plum Puddin', Purple Mouse and wow....you brought the whole town this time! Ha! Ha!"

They all laugh and Plum Puddin' introduces everyone to JB and then the four of them do the interview. After the interview is over, they tell JB about Dosi Doe being there to see Branson The Balladeer. They tell him they didn't want to talk about it during the Interview because they didn't want to ruin the surprise for her brother.

Then JB says, "I understand and I'm excited to hear how their meeting goes! I want to Interview them after they meet again!" Then, JB looks at Dosi Doe and the gang and says, "It sure is great to meet you all but, I'm sorry–I have to run. I have an Interview with Clark-Elf. He's the Official, "Elf In The Know" about anything Santa or the North Pole! If there's anything you want to know, just ask Clark."

After saying goodbye, JB takes off running but didn't realize he ran right onto the ice covered Peppermint Pond! He starts sliding across the pond and not being able to control himself, he knocks over all the elves who are skating in his path. "Oops-Sorry-Coming Through" he says as he rolls over elf after elf, but still has managed to keep his radio microphone in hand. Then, to make things worse, right in his path is Harvey the Elf who is skating. By the time they see each other, it's too late for them to get out of each other's way, and they have a huge collision! As they get up and shake off the snow, they apologize to each other and then JB slowly walks toward Clark-Elf, who is doubled over laughing at the sight he had just seen.

"JB, there's no way my Interview could top what I just saw," Clark says and laughs some more.

Then JB says to Clark, "I'm sure you'll never forget this and you'll remind me of it for the rest of my life, right?"

"Yea, that's pretty much right," Clark answers, kidding him.

"That's what I thought," says JB and they both laugh. Then JB says, "Clark, I just saw Snowdeer, Plum Puddin' and Purple Mouse and a lot of their friends and family from the Ozark Mountains. They just arrived today. I wanted to let You know in secret that they brought along a little doe who is from down south in the Branson Ozarks. Her name is Dosi Doe."

"Dosi Doe...hum..., says Clark. Her name sounds familiar and.....Wait! I know who she is! She's Branson The Balladeer's sister! I remember him talking about having a sister and mentioning the name Dosi Doe! He said they got separated a long time ago because of a big snow storm that came through Branson, the country community that he was named after. Santa found him trapped under a tree that had fallen on him when the weight of the snow made the tree break. Santa used his reindeer to pull the tree off of Branson and then to pull him out. He was hurt and was chilling and he couldn't talk at that time, so because they didn't know where he was from, Santa bundled him up and brought him here to the North Pole where he and Mrs. Claus nursed him back to health.

Once Branson got well, he just stayed here at the North Pole. His accident made him forgot for a long time who he was and where he was from. After several years, it all came back to him. I know he misses his family, especially his father and mother and Dosi Doe. He told me the night of the accident, that he knew they were also out Christmas caroling, but he didn't know if they were also stuck in the storm, or had gotten hurt like he had. He really thinks they didn't survive the snowstorm because he almost didn't, and he couldn't bear to go back and possibly find out they weren't alive, so he stayed here at the North Pole."

"Wow, is he gonna be surprised when he sees Dosi Doe and finds out his mother and father are also alive!" says JB.

"Yes, he sure will," answers Clark. Then Clark gets a great idea and says, "We'll arrange a reunion! Let's go see Santa and Mrs. Claus and make this happen!"

So, off they go across the Village to pay the Clauses a visit and tell them the good news about Dosi Doe.

13 - DOSI DOE MEETS SANTA, MRS. CLAUS & CLARK ELF

As Clark and JB arrive at the Clauses cottage, they look over and see Snowdeer, Plum Puddin', Dosi Doe and the gang walking toward them.

"Well, we meet again," says Plum Puddin' laughing.

Pinecone barks and JB introduces everyone to Clark.

After the introductions have been made, Clark looks at Dosi Doe and says, "Dosi Doe, I know your brother Branson and he always talks so highly of you." Then he explains to Dosi Doe about Branson's bad accident and because of that, he couldn't remember where he was or who his family was. He tells her how Santa saved him and brought him to the North Pole and how the Clauses took great care of him to get him back on his feet. He also tells her that Branson finally remembered it being a bad snowstorm that night and that he knew Dosi Doe and their parents were out in the storm and that he didn't know if they survived it or not. He tells Dosi Doe that Branson had told him that he couldn't bear it if he knew they hadn't survived and so he stayed at the North Pole. Then Clark says, "He will be so surprised when he sees you!"

"Oh Clark, thank you very much for telling me about Branson! How is he and where is he working?" asks Dosi Doe.

Clark answers, "He's either over at the reindeer barn feeding and watering the reindeer, or at Elf Hall singing, or he's practicing for the Christmas Production coming up at First Elfbyterian Church. He's the 'singinist' deer I've ever seen," he says and then laughs.

The gang didn't know this, but Santa and Mrs. Santa had cracked open the door enough to hear the whole conversation and they had been laughing to themselves! They already knew Dosi Doe and the gang were coming 'cause Santa could magically see them as they were saying the magic words in Plum Puddin's cabin so they could come up there. Santa had laughed when Dosi Doe thought the Sugar Snow wouldn't work, and they heard him laughing, but couldn't see him. Since Santa and Mrs. Santa knew the gang would be coming, they were already planning on throwing a great reunion party for Branson The Balladeer and Dosi Doe there at the North Pole!

Finally, Santa can't stand being quiet any longer, so he opens the door and says, "Welcome! Mrs. Claus and I heard everything and we have a plan for a surprise to pull on Branson The Balladeer!"

Dosi Doe's eyes get big and her mouth drops open at the sight of Santa and Mrs. Santa!

Then Santa smiles at her and says, "Hello Dosi Doe, it's such a pleasure to see you my dear! Your brother Branson The Balladeer loves you so much and your coming here to surprise him will make the best Christmas present he could ever receive! So, here's the plan...Mrs. Claus and I will meet with Harvey the Elf and we'll have him ask Branson to do a concert tomorrow night at Elf Hall so you can see him and surprise him!"

Then Mrs. Claus says, "It's such a pleasure to meet you Dosi Doe! I will introduce you to our helper, Tasha Mouse who works at Santa's secret underground lair. She will be happy to fit you in one of her beautiful hats to wear at Branson's concert so it will cover part of your face so he won't know it's you. You can stay with Tasha while you're here and the rest of you all can stay with Santa and I at our cottage."

14 - THE GREAT REUNION
AT THE NORTH POLE KINGDOM

So, they head over to Santa's underground lair, and after they go down the secret staircase, they find Tasha Mouse working and getting ready for Christmas. Tasha, being the kind hearted lady she is, greets everyone and then takes Dosi Doe to her private living quarters where they go through her hat closet to pick out the perfect hat for Dosi Doe to wear to her brother's concert. The hat she picks has a silk cloth that comes down the sides of her face and ties at the neck.

"Branson will never know it's you," says Tasha.

"Great! That's exactly what I want!" answers Dosi Doe.

"Let's go back to the gang and show them your new look Dosi Doe," says Tasha.

"Ok," replies Dosi Doe and off they go back to Santa and the gang to show off her new fashion accessory.

When they get back, Santa observes the new hat and then breaks into a hearty laugh, making his belly shake and he says, "HO-HO-HO! O Branson will never know!" and then laughs again. The rest of the gang join in laughing with Santa and Pinecone starts barking.

"It looks perfect dear," says Mrs. Claus and everyone agrees that it is the perfect disguise.

Then Santa says, "Dosi Doe, would you like a personal guided tour of my underground lair?"

"O, yes sir Santa," answers Dosi Doe. So Santa walks them through his underground museum, showing them his work shop, his treasure chests of gold, silver and jewels, and picture after picture of friends he has made throughout the world.

"Santa, how did you get all of this?" asks Dosi Doe.

Santa replies, "My dear, I've been around for hundreds of years and through the years I've collected things from every country in the world. I've eaten more cookies and drank more milk than anyone ever has or ever will!" and then he laughs. "I've even taken trips during the year when it wasn't the Christmas Season. I've disguised myself in regular clothes and trimmed my beard and wore a top hat. I would use my Sugar Snow magic dust to surround my sleigh and the reindeer and make them disappear 'till I would get back. Then we'd take off real fast hoping no one saw us! I have to admit I did get some funny looks that one year when I went

35

into the bakery and asked for Noel nut balls and hot cocoa in the middle of July! HO-HO-HO! But most of the time I was able to fool people, just like you're going to fool your brother Branson tomorrow night," Santa says with a laugh.

After hours of looking at Santa's treasures, they reach the big long staircase that leads them above ground. As they come to the top of the stairs, they find a door that leads right into the Reindeer Barn. Santa opens the door and they see Harvey, The Reindeer Preparation Elf racing around laughing and cuttin' up with his fellow elves.

When Harvey sees Santa and the gang he says, 'Well, Ha-Ha-Ha-Ho-Ho-Ho! Look who I found from down below!"

They all laugh and Santa says, "Harvey, we need your help. This is Dosi Doe-Branson The Balladeer's sister from......"

"Sister?" Harvey asks. Then he gets a big grin on his face and runs up to Dosi Doe and says, "Dosi Doe, your brother talks to me about you all the time! Nice to meet you Miss Doe. Well, Ha-Ha-Ha-Ho-Ho-Ho! Today I met Branson's Dosi Doe!"

Then Santa continues, "Harvey, we need you to ask Branson The Balladeer to put on a Concert tomorrow night at Elf Hall with Josh, Dale & Melody Elf. Dosi Doe is going to dress in disguise and surprise him!"

"Great! I will get right on it Santa," says Harvey and off he goes to set the Concert up with Branson.

"Please make it for 7 o'clock Harvey," hollers Santa, hoping Harvey heard him before he got too far away.

"Yes Sir Santa," replies Harvey as his voice trails off in the distance.

As Harvey is racing through the Reindeer Barn on his way to find Branson, he walks by Santa's magic trunk of Sugar Snow. He wants to play in the snow, but decides he'd better be good. He searches the barn for Branson the Balladeer, but he doesn't see him, so he hollers for him. He hears Branson holler back. He runs up to him. Harvey wants so badly to tell him the news about his sister coming to see him perform, but he knows that he can't tell him. So, he just asks, "What are you doing today? Have you written any new songs?"

"Yes, replies Branson. But lately I've been thinking so much about my father Branson, my mother Mary and my sister Dosi Doe that I haven't been writing as much. I still wonder if they are alive and survived that bad snowstorm. I will always be thankful to Santa and his Team of reindeer for saving my life."

"Yes, that's for sure Branson," says Harvey. Then he continues, "You know Branson, your sister could turn up someday when you least expect it."

"That's what I pray for Harvey and if I see her, I'll sing to her the song my daddy Reuben Branson and I wrote for her".

Then Harvey asks, "Branson, Santa has asked if you would please put on a Christmas Concert tomorrow night at Elf Hall."

"Really? At Elf Hall tomorrow?" asks Branson.

"Yes, tomorrow night and would you make it for 7 o'clock please?" asks Harvey.

"Yes! I would be honored to do it! I have so many new songs I've written that I want to introduce to all at the North Pole Village!" answers an excited Branson the Balladeer.

"Santa also requested for Josh, Melody and Dale Elf to perform too. Would you ask them please?" asks Harvey.

"Yes, and at 7 o'clock we'll have a show," answers Branson.

Harvey says, "Thanks Branson, see you tomorrow night," and off he races back to Santa, Dosi Doe and the gang. When he arrives, he's out of breath, but with an excited voice he tells them that Branson agreed to do a show that next night with Josh, Melody and Dale Elf at 7 o'clock at Elf Hall.

The gang cheers and Santa says, "Let's all go back to the cottage and see if we can talk Mrs. Claus into fixing something to eat," and then he winks at Mrs. Claus. Then, he looks at Plum Puddin' and says, "Plum Puddin', did you bring Plum Pudding this time?"

Plum Puddin' drops his head and replies, "No sir Santa. I'm so sorry. We were so excited to come see you and bring Dosi Doe that I completely forgot! You know, something has to be pretty important for me to forget Plum Pudding!"

They all laugh and Santa says, "HO-HO-HO! That's Ok Plum. I understand and you are right. Dosi Doe is pretty special, but I expect TWO jars of Plum Pudding the next time you visit! HO-HO-HO!" he laughs and holds up two fingers to make his point. Then he shakes his head and says, "Only joking my friend, you are off the hook!"

Santa turns to Mrs. Claus and says, "Dear, after you fix something for our travelers, I will treat everyone to Dunne's Christmas Buns for desert!" Everyone cheers and Mrs. Santa says, "Yes, Dear, I would love to fix our special friends something to eat, and your desert idea will work perfectly."

Then Santa sends Plum Puddin', Snowdeer and Purple Mouse to get the desert while Mrs. Santa prepares supper.

After a wonderful meal and special desert, they settle in for many hours relaxing at Santa and Mrs. Santa's cottage. They watch the fireplace burning and listen to Christmas carols playing and they talk about Snowdeer, Plum Puddin' and Purple Mouse and their trips to the North Pole. As they are all getting sleepy and starting to nod, Santa says, "The hour is getting late and I need to go back to my secret lair to check on some things before I head out with the reindeer to deliver gifts. Dosi Doe, please come with me and I'll take you to stay with Tasha Mouse."

When Santa realizes that he and Mrs. Claus don't have enough beds for the rest of the gang, he laughs a big, HO-HO-HO and says, "We don't have enough beds. Plum Puddin', Snowdeer and Purple Mouse, you stay here at the cottage with me and Mrs. Santa. Everyone else, please stay at The Peppermint Suites, at our special chalets over by Mews Mountain. We'll all meet here at our cottage at noon tomorrow for lunch and then I'll give you a tour of the North Pole Village. After that, we'll head over to Elf Hall and enjoy the big Concert tomorrow night! Have a great night and see you tomorrow. HO-HO-HO!"

The gang tells Santa and Mrs. Claus thank you and goodnight and then the tired but happy group go their separate ways for the night. All of them are excited about the events of the next day and wonder if they will be able to sleep.

As the new day dawns, Dosi Doe's eyes pop wide open and her thoughts turn to her brother Branson The Balladeer.

Tasha wakes up excited too and the girls start talking and giggling about the hat that Dosi Doe will wear to hide from her brother. Tasha has many stories about Santa and how great it is to work with him while Dosi Doe shares stories about her life in the Ozark Mountains. They meet the gang promptly at noon and have a wonderful meal prepared by Mrs. Claus.

After eating, Plum Puddin' goes to lay down to take a nap but Mama Rose Marie says, "Hey Plum, where are you going?"

"Just to take a little nap Mama. I'm sleepy and full," answers Plum Puddin.

"The nap isn't gonna happen," says Snowdeer laughing.

"You're gonna go with the rest of us and tour the Village," says Purple Mouse also laughing.

"Oh, Ok," says Plum and they all head out the door.

"We have a lot of special people to meet today," says Santa.

As they go to the middle of the North Pole Village, they see Strike The Bell standing there quietly.

"Hello Strike, how are you today?" asks Santa.

Strike just rings his bell in reply as the gang walk past him and goes around the block. Plum Puddin', Snowdeer and Purple Mouse however, stayed with Strike so they could talk to their friend. When he sees it is ok to talk, Strike says, "How are you my friends? I know you're busy with your tour with Santa and your family and friends, but come back when you have time to talk some more. I wish I could to talk to everybody, but the fact that I can talk is a secret that I just can't share with everyone."

"Ok, we'll be back Strike," says Plum Puddin'. So, they tell him goodbye and rejoin Santa and the gang, and continue walking and seeing the enchanting sights of the North Pole Village.

As they come up to Mews Mountain, they see Hew Mew the cat. "Hey Hew, how are you?" asks Purple Mouse.

"Doing great Purple Mouse," answers Hew.

"Would you and your family please sing for us Hew?" asks Purple Mouse.

Hew answers, "Yes, we would love to sing for you."

Then Daddy Darrell says, "We have heard so much about you all. We're looking forward to this!"

Then Hew says, "Thank You. Let me get my mother Deborah Lew and my dad Bartholomew and the rest of the family."

As Hew goes to get his mother and father and all of his many brothers and sisters, Purple Mouse laughs and says, "This could take a while 'cause there's a whole lot of mews."

In a few minutes, the gang gasps as they see at least 100 cats running out the windows, through the doors, out the chimneys, off the roof top. With the cats racing toward them, Maroon and Orchid Mouse freeze in surprise. Hew sees this and roars with laughter and says, "Don't worry, you are perfectly safe with us. We would never do anything to harm you. And besides if we did and Santa found out......"

Purple Mouse finishes the sentence by saying, "That would be 'Cat-a-strophic'!"

Everyone laughs and Hew looks at Purple Mouse and says, "How did you know?" and then laughs again.

Purple Mouse rolls his eyes and then Hew Mew looks at his family and asks, "Are you ready?" They answer yes, and then Hew looks at his Dad Bartholomew and asks, "Daddy, would you hit the key on the pitch pipe please?"

Bartholomew nods and smiles and then gives them the key on the pitch pipe.

Then, Deborah Lew counts off the song, "The Good Mews of Christmas." As they begin to sing in perfect harmony, everyone in the group stands there in awe listening intently.

Then, all of a sudden, Santa's magical Sugar Snow comes flying over them. The Snow flies up and over them. Then it comes down and swirls around each one of them. As the Sugar Snow comes up close, they can see some snowflakes smiling. Some are looking mischievous. Some are laughing. And some even brush up against Snowdeer and the gang giving them a cold feeling and making them shiver. All of the gang are amazed at the beautiful song and the beautiful lights and smiles of the Sugar Snow show. When the song ends, the Sugar Snow heads back to the North Pole's pole and to Santa's special Sugar Snow box in the barn.

"What a beautiful job on your song," says Snowdeer.

"Thank you" answers Bartholomew. "We love singing together and are happy to share our song with you."

"I want to thank you all very much too! It was just as beautiful as the first time I heard it," says Purple Mouse.

"You are welcome my friend. You weren't nervous like you were when we met you first time last year." says Deborah Lew and then she laughs.

"That's for sure Deborah Lew. Talk about being out-numbered!" says Purple Mouse. They all laugh knowing what happened the first time they met when he was one mouse among at least 100 cats.

Then, Mewlinda Mew says, "You need to make a trip to see us every Christmas. And next time-don't forget to bring the presents!"

They all laugh and Plum Puddin' says, "Thank You all very much. We will come back again for sure."

After they all say their goodbyes, they go by and visit with all the folks at Body by Dorn & Co, Marquart's Molasses, Krull's Confectionary and Plummer's Reindeer Hardware. They stop by Dunne's Christmas Buns again and have delicious rolls and red velvet cake. As time rolls on, they see more and more people and make new friends.

Then, all of a sudden, Santa looks at the big clock in the middle of the North Pole Village and gives a big, "HO-HO-HO! 40 minutes 'till the Show!"

They're all amazed at how fast the time had gone and Dosi Doe says, "Let's go over to Elf Hall! I can't wait to see my brother!" They all start heading that way, led by Santa. They are eager to hear Branson The Balladeer, Melody, Dale and Josh Elf perform, and are promptly seated at 6:30.

The curtain goes up exactly at 7 o'clock and Josh Elf introduces Melody and Dale Elf and himself, After each sings their own special song, Josh introduces Branson The Balladeer. He comes out and starts singing. Dosi Doe is thrilled to see her brother perform.

At intermission, as the lights come up, Dosi Doe mistakenly takes off her hat. They are sitting close enough to the stage that Branson The Balladeer sees her and their eyes meet. He stops and stares at her, speechless.

She too is at a loss for words, but Santa, who is sitting by Dosi Doe, stands up and announces to all, "Branson The Balladeer, please make welcome your sister Dosi Doe."

A great rush of "Aaahs" followed by clapping erupts throughout the room. Everyone rises to their feet, and gives them a standing ovation. There is not a dry eye in Elf Hall. Then, Branson invites Dosi Doe to come to the stage. They run toward each other and hug for a couple of minutes. The crowd tearfully watches the love of a sister and brother as they are reunited.

Once he regains his composure, Branson says to Dosi Doe, "We are never ever gonna be separated again and that's a promise!" The crowd breaks out into applause and they hug again. Then, Branson The Balladeer tells the story about how an Ozark Mountain snowstorm separated them at Christmas and how he was pinned down by a tree that had fallen on him. He tells how he was almost completely buried in the snow and how Santa found him and saved him by bringing him to the North Pole. He tells the audience how he didn't go back to the Ozarks because he thought his family had also gotten buried in the snow. So he just stayed at the North Pole and made a new life there.

He then tells about the song their father Reuben Branson and himself wrote for her. He puts his arm around her, he sings the song and it brings down the house! They hug again and Dosi Doe says, "I'm gonna go sit down 'cause I don't think I can take any more excitement tonight!" Everyone breaks out in laughter and Dosi Doe goes back to the audience while a very happy Branson The Balladeer finishes the night's program.

15 - SANTA'S QUESTION FOR SNOWDEER

After the Show, Santa and Mrs. Santa invite Dosi Doe, Branson The Balladeer and all the gang to come to their cottage for cookies, hot chocolate and to hear stories from Branson The Balladeer and Dosi Doe. They talk way into the night, telling story after story of things that have happened in their lives since they were separated and also sharing stories about their early lives together in Branson. All the gang is so excited to hear their stories that no one wants to go to sleep.

Then out of the blue, Santa looks at Snowdeer and says, "Snowdeer, I have a very special question for you."

"What's that Santa," replies Snowdeer.

Santa says, "Well, I've known you for quite a while now. I know how much you love Christmas and how your Christmas wish one year was to help us out here at the North Pole by pulling my sleigh. It worked out perfect when the reindeer got sick."

"Yes Sir, that was one of the greatest adventures of my whole entire life Santa!" says Snowdeer.

Santa continues, "Well, Snowdeer, with there are getting to be so many people and animals in the world, I could sure use your help again. Would you like to be onboard here at the North Pole delivering presents on Christmas Eve? And then during the year you could fly around the world spreading peace and good will to everyone as my ambassador." Snowdeer becomes speechless and Santa breaks in and says, "You don't have to make a decision tonight, but please let me know as soon as you..."

Snowdeer begins jumping for joy and says, "Santa, I would be honored to be your ambassador! When do we start?"

Santa gets a big grin on his face, leans back and gives a big, "HO-HO-HO, I was hoping you'd say so! Snowdeer, as of tonight, I'm making you a full time member of the North Pole Kingdom Flyers!"

"Wow! What an honor! I will always do my very best for you Santa!" says an overjoyed Snowdeer.

Then Santa jokes and says, "I know you will, 'cause that's why I choose you...my little deer," and they all laugh. Santa continues, "We can start training you tomorrow, but tonight I have something to show everyone. Follow me." So, Santa lights a lantern and leads the gang back down to his secret underground lair. Santa takes them to a big wooden door and then asks Harvey to open it. After he does, the gang gasps as they see a beautiful decorated sleigh with the initials SD on it!

Snowdeer's mouth drops open wide as he stands staring at a sleigh that's been custom built for him and even detailed with his initials on it! He looks at Santa and says, "Santa, I don't know what to say except, Thank you Sir."

Santa again gives a big, "HO-HO-HO" and says, "You said all you needed to say when you said you would be my ambassador Snowdeer."

Then, Snowdeer's parents, Jim-Buck and Deerlores walk up to Snowdeer and hug their son and give him their blessing for becoming one of Santa's team. Jim-Buck jokes at Snowdeer by asking, "Son, you will come to visit your mother and I, won't you?

Snowdeer gets an ornery look on his face and says, "You bet I will Daddy, and if you're good, I might bring you something!"

Then, Deerlores joins in and jokes at Jim-Buck saying, "Jim-Buck? Good? Well my DEER husband, from what I've seen so far, I don't see you getting anything this year!" Jim-Buck and everyone laughs.

Santa, seeing the love of this family says, "Snowdeer, you can still live part of your life down in the Ozarks at Doe Run with your family and friends and when I need you, I'll send someone from the North Pole to get you."

"That sounds great Santa! Thank you so much. I really do appreciate it," says Snowdeer.

Then Santa says, "You're sure welcome. All of the North Pole will be excited when they hear the great news about you!" Then turning around to all of the gang, Santa says, "Well my friends, it's been a long eventful day so, "HO-HO-HO! It's off to bed we go! Let's get a good night's sleep before tomorrow's busy day!"

They all agree and they start walking to their sleep quarters, excited about what all is going to happen with Snowdeer and his new mission with Santa!

16 - SNOWDEER'S TRAINING DAY

The next morning bright and early, Snowdeer wakes to find Santa and Mrs. Santa already up and busy with their day. The smell of hot cocoa, chocolate chip cookies and freshly baked Dunne's Christmas buns fill the air of the cottage, making Snowdeer smile. He looks across the room and sees Plum Puddin' and Purple Mouse still sleeping. Then he remembers that today is his special training day. Not being able to stay in bed any longer, he jumps up and goes over between their beds and hollers, "Plum Puddin'! Purple Mouse! Wake up!" They awake and then yawn and stretch and Snowdeer says, "Today's the day! My training day!"

"Oh yea!" they answer and then bounce out of their beds. They rush out to find Santa and Mrs. Santa sitting at the breakfast table drinking hot cocoa and planning their day. After a great breakfast and hearing some of Santa's tales of his travels Santa grins at Snowdeer, Plum Puddin' and Purple Mouse and says, "Well, it's Day 1 of Snowdeer Training. Everyone up to it?"

"Yes Sir," the three of them reply and off to Santa's lair they go.

Tasha Mouse and Dosi Doe are already up and Tasha has been showing her how to make hats and clothes and other things that will be used for presents to fulfill wishes of children and animals around the world. As they hear Santa, Snowdeer, Plum Puddin' and Purple Mouse coming down the stairs, they run over to meet them and to give them a big hug. When Purple Mouse sees Tasha Mouse, he immediately blushes the brightest purple he has ever blushed.

Santa, having seen it, starts to belly laugh and Plum Puddin' says, "Some things never change, do they Purple Mouse!" That doesn't help Purple Mouse at all and he blushes even more and looks down in embarrassment shaking his head.

All of a sudden, they hear footsteps coming down Santa's secret lair staircase. Darrell, Rose Marie, Jim-Buck, Deerlores, Maroon, Orchid, Terrie Young Deer and the others walk up to Santa and the gang, and with big smiles on their faces, they all greet each other with a happy, "Good Morning."

Then Santa walks over and puts his hand on Snowdeer's back and says, "Snowdeer, this is a very special day for you and all of us here at the North Pole. There will be some training for you, but with the love God gave you for children, adults and animals, you are a natural and it won't seem like work at all to you. You will need to check regularly with Russ and Bev Elf because they will be meeting with the elves during the year to make sure the toys are made and ready on time. Harvey, The Reindeer Preparation Elf will make sure there's plenty of Sugar Snow handy to dust on you, the sleigh and the others who will be flying with you. With the many trips you'll be making during the year, we want you to be in tip-top shape and have the best help you can to make sure everything runs right on schedule. You'll be going around the world many times and you will need a lot of help. We're all gonna help you, aren't we gang?"

The gang starts cheering and clapping for Snowdeer and pledging their devotion to helping him meet all his upcoming tasks.

The reality of what Santa is asking of him starts to sink in and Snowdeer asks Santa, "Who's going to ride in my sleigh and who's going to fly it with me?"

Santa answers, "Snowdeer, I want as many of your family and friends that are here right now to be ready to help you when you need help. Also, if during the year you would need any of my reindeer to run with you, just ask and I know they would be more than willing to help."

Snowdeer smiles and says, "Oh wow Santa, thanks!" Then Snowdeer looks at Jim-Buck & Deerlores and asks, "Mama and Daddy, will you go with me sometimes?"

Jim-Buck looks at him and says, "Yes, we would be happy to go with you Son,".

Deerlores says, "I wouldn't miss it for the world. I'm here for You Snowdeer."

"You can for sure count me in Snowdeer," says Dosi Doe.

Branson the Balladeer says, "Snowdeer, you are perfect for the job and I'm with you all the way my friend. Oh, by the way, Is it ok if I sing sometimes while we travel?"

Everyone laughs and Snowdeer says, "You bet Branson. We can carol all the way!"

Then Plum Puddin' says, "Snowdeer, I would be honored to ride along and pass out gifts for you. And then during the year, if you would want, I could go along and talk with people and spread good cheer with you and maybe even take along some Plum Pudding, if that's alright."

Snowdeer laughs and says, "Yes Plum! I need your help and please feel free to bring along as much Plum Pudding as you would like!" Then Snowdeer's face lights up with an idea and he says, "Matter of fact, we might even take along hundreds of jars of Plum Pudding to hand out to people and animals around the world, and not just at Christmas, but during the entire year!"

Plum Puddin' smiles real big and thanks Snowdeer and then Purple Mouse says, "I for sure want to help you out Snowdeer. Even if you do tease me about turnin' purple!"

Snowdeer laughs and then one by one, everyone tells Snowdeer they want to help.

Then Santa says, "Harvey can come along and help and we also have our very special elves, Rene Elf and Elva Elf who can write up your Christmas lists and then go along and check off their names after you have delivered to them."

45

"That sounds great Santa," says Snowdeer.

Then Santa walks over to a special work room in the back of his lair where elves are busy working and he hollers, "Rene and Elva Elf, are you here?"

Then he hears two voices saying, "Yes Sir, Santa, we're here."

Santa says, "Wonderful, would you both please come with me?" Then Santa walks back to Snowdeer and the gang with Rene and Elva Elf and he says, "I want to introduce you to some friends of mine that will soon be friends of yours." Santa then introduces Rene and Elva Elf to the gang and then tells them that Rene and Elva built Snowdeer's sleigh!

A very thankful Snowdeer looks at them and says, "Thank you very much Rene and Elva! You did a wonderful job on my sleigh!"

"It was our pleasure," Rene says and Elva says, "We had to keep it a secret. None of the other elves knew you were getting it."

Snowdeer and the gang go over and hug them both and tell them how they appreciate their hard work. Santa then asks them if they would help make a list of children, adults and animals and the gifts that Snowdeer should give to them.

They both get excited and Rene Elf says, "Yes Sir, Santa, we would be happy to help Snowdeer."

Elva Elf looks at Snowdeer and says, "We are at your service Snowdeer. Any friend of Santa is a friend of ours."

Then Santa says, "Ladies, we also need your help with something else. Would you please go with Snowdeer on some of his trips to check off the list of the people, animals and gifts as Snowdeer delivers them?"

"O Yes Santa, we would enjoy that," says Rene and Elva says, "We have wanted to travel on a sleigh for years and now we'll get to! Thank you Santa!"

Then Santa says, "Wonderful! HO-HO-HO! Rene and Elva's gonna go!"

Everyone cheers and the excitement builds as everyone looks forward to Snowdeer's first flight.

17 - BACK TO PLUM PUDDIN'S CABIN

Santa, being happy with how the first day of training had gone, says to Snowdeer and the gang, "That is all the training for today. You are free to do what you want."

Then Snowdeer says, "Well, I reckon we'd better get back to Plum Puddin's cabin and tell all the others at Doe Run, Knob Lick and Possum Holler what's been happening lately. We've had some big changes, haven't we?" and then he laughs.

"Yes, we all sure have, but especially you, Snowdeer," answers Santa.

Then Plum Puddin' says, "I'll go to your cottage Santa and get our Magical Jars and then meet you all in the middle of the North Pole village over by Strike The Bell. We can tell everyone bye from there and then head back to Knob Lick."

So, Plum Puddin' heads to Santa's cottage and finds Snowdeer's, Purple Mouse's and his own Magical Jars. He meets the gang at the middle of the North Pole Village and puts the jars into his friends hands. By now a big crowd has gathered to watch them take off. The three friends look at Strike The Bell and tell him goodbye. They know he can't say anything, but he gives a special nod. After telling all goodbye, they firmly hold onto their jars, and all of the gang says, "HO-HO-HO! OFF TO PLUM PUDDIN'S CABIN WE GO!"

Then Strike The Bell starts ringing his bell and the Sugar Snow starts flying out of Santa's reindeer barn and also from over at the North Pole's Pole. It circles each one of them and then whisks them away and within minutes they're back at Plum Puddin's cabin.

"Whew, that was quick!" says Mama Rose Marie.

Orchid Mouse answers and says, "Yes, it sure was! We gotta do it again sometime!"

They all laugh and Snowdeer says, "I promise you that you will get your chance. Now to find my sister and brothers. They'll be so excited when they find out they're going to Santa's to deliver gifts!"

"Yes, they sure will. Let's go find them," says Purple Mouse. So off they go and soon they find Snowdeer's sister Rosie, and his brothers Deerell, Antler & Longnose picking nuts and berries in the Doe Run woods.

"Hello you all!" says Snowdeer with great excitement.

"Where have you been? We've been worried about you," asks Deerell.

Snowdeer answers, "Just wait 'till you hear this! I've got great news to tell you!" Then he tells them the story of how they went to the North Pole and how

47

Santa had a sleigh built especially for him so he could deliver gifts around the world and be a special ambassador for Santa. Rosie, Deerell, Antler and Longnose just stand there looking at Snowdeer in shock with their mouths wide open, not knowing what to say. Snowdeer then says, "Now to the part that includes you."

"Includes us?" asks Rosie. Snowdeer shakes his head and answers,

"Yes! Santa said he needs you all to help pull my sleigh. At least on special occasions. Would you like to help?"

"Yes! Count me in," says Antler and then Longnose, Rosie and Deerell chime in and say they would love to help him out too.

Snowdeer says, "Great! I'll be leaving soon to go back to the North Pole and I will take you back with me. What fun we're gonna have taking out the sleigh on trips during the year as well as at Christmas time to spread peace and goodwill to everyone we meet!"

"That's wonderful! Sharing the Christmas Spirit all during the year! I'm always sad to see Christmas end, but now we can celebrate it every day!" says Longnose.

"Yes, that's right," agrees Snowdeer. Then he remembers Dosi Doe and Branson The Balladeer had come to Possum Holler with him and he says, "Come with me to Plum Puddin's cabin. I have a surprise for you."

So, they all head to the cabin and see Branson The Balladeer and meet Dosi Doe and then hear Snowdeer tell the story about how Branson the Balladeer and Dosi Doe had gotten separated and then met up again at the North Pole. Snowdeer's sister and brothers are amazed at how they found each other, and how they look forward to flying Snowdeer's sleigh with them.

Daddy Darrell laughs and says, "Our family keeps getting bigger and bigger. Well, the more the merrier!"

Pinecone walks over to Plum Puddin' and lays down in front of him and rolls over on his back so Plum Puddin' can scratch his belly.

Then Purple Mouse says, "Oh to be so lucky. To just lay down and get a good scratchin'. I could sure use a good back scratch right now."

Maroon jokes and says, "Well, you need to ask Tasha Mouse to scratch your back the next time you're at the North Pole! I'm sure she would do it!" After saying that, Purple Mouse's face turns a bright purple and he just shakes his head while everyone laughs.

18 - SANTA'S NORTH POLE KINGDOM FLYERS

Snowdeer, his family, and all the gang start talking about what they want to do to help Snowdeer. Terrie Young Deer says, "Snowdeer, if you would like, Niangua and I can pick fruit, nuts and berries and make horns-of-plenty for you to take to the North Pole to distribute to families around the world at Christmas time and also during the year."

Snowdeer's uncles Ken-Buck and Mark-Buck offer to make Pine Cone Chips for him to take on his travels, and Todd says, "I would be happy to use Glister and my wagon and pick up the Pine Cone Chips and the horns-of-plenty and take everything over to Plum Puddin's cabin. Then Plum Puddin', Snowdeer and Purple Mouse can use their Magical Jars Santa gave them and take themselves and the Christmas goodies to the North Pole."

Darrell and Jim-Buck say they can build wooden toys and Rose Marie and Deerlores say they can sew and stitch things for young and old alike to contribute to Snowdeer's trips. Everyone is excited to be a part.

Snowdeer thanks them and says, "I wish we could go back to the North Pole and fly out tonight to take gifts to people and animals."

Right after he says that, they all hear a wonderful familiar voice in the distance saying, "HO-HO-HO!" They look up in the sky and see Santa flying toward them with all his reindeer and Sugar Snow swirling all around! The whole gang is thrilled to see him and they gasp in amazement, but they're also puzzled as to why he would be coming so soon.

After Santa lands his sleigh, Snowdeer asks, "Santa-Sir, What are you doing here so early?"

Santa laughs and replies, "I'm delivering the first gift of the year and it's for you Snowdeer. Look up."

As they all look up, they see a huge cloud of Sugar Snow covering something wrapped in a big Christmas bow. The Sugar Snow lowers it to the ground and then clears a path for Snowdeer to come see his surprise. Snowdeer's eyes light up when he sees what it is, and he says, "You brought my sleigh!"

"That's right Snowdeer," says Santa, "I wanted to bring it to you so you could take it to the North Pole when you come back. This would also give you some sleigh flying practice! HO-HO-HO! And Another reason I came is because I wanted to ask your family if they would like to join my special group, Santa's North Pole

Kingdom Flyers!" Then Santa looks at Snowdeer's family and asks, "Would you like to become members of Santa's North Pole Kingdom Flyers?"

All of Snowdeer's family gives a hearty, "Yes Sir!"

Then Santa gets a big grin on his face and looking Snowdeer right in the eyes, he says, "I also came 'cause I have another very important question and it is for you my friend. Snowdeer, now that you have your own sleigh, I want you to take the reins and drive it instead of pulling it. Will you do that please?"

Snowdeer's mouth drops open and his eyes get real big, and with a surprised look on his face, he says, "Yes Sir Santa! I would love to do that! Thank you!"

Then Santa says, "HO-HO-HO! Let's get harnessed up and go! We have a busy night ahead of us, my little deer!" Everyone laughs with joy, and Santa says, "Mrs. Claus is already counting on us for supper and then we'll have an evening of fun and learning more about the North Pole. It looks like you're going to be spending a lot of time there! HO-HO-HO!" As Santa looks at all of the gang, it dawns on him that there isn't enough room to fit everyone in his and Snowdeer's sleighs. Then he gets an idea and he says, "Whoever wants to ride on any of my reindeer or on Snowdeer's family, please feel free to hop on. That way everyone can go." So, everyone who doesn't ride in a sleigh picks a reindeer or deer to ride on and Snowdeer, Plum Puddin' & Purple Mouse grab their Magical Jars. Santa asks the Sugar Snow to circle the group and then asks the gang to say along with him the magical words that will send them off to the North Pole. Then all together, Santa and the gang shout, "SUGAR SNOW! SUGAR SNOW! OFF TO THE NORTH POLE WE GO!" And at that command, the Sugar Snow swirls around everyone, and off they fly with Snowdeer holding the reins driving his sleigh, with his family flying it, followed by Santa and his sleigh and reindeer!

What a wonderful night it was for Santa, Snowdeer and his family and friends, who are now members of Santa's North Pole Kingdom Flyers.

19 - BAYBERRY BAY

After they arrive at the North Pole, Ken-Buck and Mark-Buck look around at the sights and notice the big tower of CMAS Radio Station. Ken-Buck says, "Whew, we sure got here fast!"

Santa, hearing their conversation says, "Your Pine Cone Chip Company is about to take off as fast as the Sugar Snow that got you here!" They all laugh, but Ken-Buck and Mark-Buck look at each other wondering what Santa meant. Then Santa continues, "The reason I say that is because I want to ask you an important question. The Krull's Confectionary candy kitchen elves and I have talked already and I want to ask a question. Would you consider going back and forth to the North Pole throughout the year bringing the nuts, chocolate and waffle cone mix to us? Then, you and the kitchen elves can work together to make Pine Cone Chips right here at the North Pole. Snowdeer and I could it deliver around the world on our routes. We can add them to our gifts to make the presents extra special!"

"YES! We would be honored to do it Santa!" both Ken-Buck and Mark-Buck shout.

"Then it's a deal! Pine Cone Chips is now the official candy of the North Pole Kingdom!" Santa declares.

All the gang cheers and Ken-Buck jokingly says to Snowdeer, "Little nephew, when you're not roamin' around the world, I expect you, Purple Mouse and Plum Puddin' to be back with us pickin' lots and lots of nuts to put in the Pine Cone Chips!"

Snowdeer jokes back and says, "Uncle Ken, I'm gonna have so much Sugar Snow flyin' around me that you'll never catch me to put me to work!"

They all laugh and continue walking around the North Pole Village. Santa takes the Buck brothers over to see Mrs. Santa, Harvey the Elf, Josh, Amber, Lilly Kay Elf, Ilsa Marie Elf, Strike the Bell, Hew Mew and his cat family and many, many others. When they go down to Santa's underground lair, they meet Rene & Elva Elf and Tasha Mouse. Purple Mouse once again blushes his usual bright purple at the sight of Tasha. The Buck brothers look at him thinking "What in the world did you just do" and then they burst into laughter.

Purple Mouse looks at everyone and then looks down and says, "I know, I know. Don't say a word," which brings everyone to laugh again.

After they go back upstairs, they have the deer pull Snowdeer's beautiful new sleigh to the Reindeer Barn. As they bring it inside, Harvey Elf leads them to a big closet especially made for it. Snowdeer gets a big smile on his face as he sees his name in big letters on the front doors.

He thanks Santa for it and Santa says, "Snowdeer, the Elves built this for you because they believe in you and they're excited about what you will be doing here at the North Pole." Then Santa motions his hand forward and says, "Snowdeer, I have something else to show you." As the gang walk out the door they see in the distance a huge body of water. It is completely frozen over and elves are skating on it. "That's Bayberry Bay," says Santa, "Let's go over and see it."

So they all walk over and as they approach the shoreline, Snowdeer and all gasp and Snowdeer says, "It smells like Bayberry!" Santa replies, "Yes, it does my friend. I wanted to have your office next to it so you could enjoy the scent anytime you are here."

"My office?" asks Snowdeer.

"Yes, your very own office," answers Santa. Then Santa tells everyone to look over to the right and then he says, "See that cottage?"

"Yes sir," answers Snowdeer. "Well, that is your office and your home away from home when you're on duty here," says Santa. "You will have enough room for Plum Puddin', Purple Mouse and whoever else you would want to come and help you in your travels. Rene and Elva Elf will be here on a regular basis to help with your lists of people and animals to see and their locations. There are even enough rooms for Jim-Buck and Deerlores and your family to stay. If we run out of room, we'll just send them over to the Peppermint Suites!"

An overwhelmed Snowdeer says, "Thank you Santa-Thank you very much."

As Santa, Snowdeer and the gang walk across Bayberry Bay and come up to Snowdeer's cottage, they see two candles dressed in uniforms standing at attention at the cottage entrance. Santa looks at them and says, "HO-HO-HO! Taper and Tallow! How are you my friends?" The two candles square their shoulders and smile and greet Santa back. Then Santa turns to Snowdeer and says, "Taper and Tallow are on special assignment from me to be your personal assistants. They will be at your beck and call anytime you are here. They will work closely with Rene and Elva Elf in mapping out your routes on your very own Magical Map."

"Hello Mr. Snowdeer, nice to meet you," says Taper.

And then Tallow says, "Hello Mr. Snowdeer, it is a pleasure to serve you."

"Hello Taper and Tallow, it's an honor to meet you and I look forward to working with you both," says Snowdeer.

"Taper and Tallow, please unlock the door and let our honorary deer inside. I'm anxious for him and all the gang to see his new headquarters," says Santa.

So, they unlock the door and everyone goes inside. As they enter the first room, they marvel at the beautiful craftsmanship of the cottage. Santa walks over to Snowdeer's desk that has SNOWDEER carved on the front and picks up a bell that is sitting on it. Then he says, "Snowdeer, here's a special magical bell I made just for you. If you need me anytime, all you have to do is ring it. I will be able to hear it no matter where I am in the world. If you ever need my help, I will be right there to help you."

"Thank you Santa, it just keeps gettin' better and better! I promise to be the best I can be for you Sir," answers Snowdeer.

Santa smiles and nods and says, "I am convinced you will be Snowdeer." Then Santa motions again with his hand and says, "Come on, let's tour the rest of the cottage."

So they go from one room to another and as they go into the kitchen, Rene Elf says, "We'll spend a lot of time here because I love to cook."

Elva Elf says, "Let me know the things you enjoy eating and we'll fix 'em for you Snowdeer."

Tallow joins in and says, "If you want, Taper and I can use your kitchen table to chart your trips as well as to eat on. That way we can make sure none of us will miss any meals!"

They all laugh and Snowdeer wholeheartedly agrees and says, "Ok, that's what we'll do 'cause I like to eat too!"

After the tour is finished, Santa makes a suggestion, "Why don't we all go skating on Bayberry Bay?"

"Yea!" the gang replies and off they go. For the next few hours they skate and enjoy the beauty and the smell of Bayberry Bay.

Later, after they are tired from skating, Santa says to the gang, "Let's go over to my cottage, see Mrs. Claus and eat the meal she has been preparing. She's really been looking forward to cooking for you!" So they head over to Santa's cottage and Pinecone rings the doorbell with his nose.

Mrs. Claus answers the door in her Christmas apron and with a twinkle in her eyes she says, "Welcome everyone! Come on in and make yourself at home. Supper is almost done!" The group starts filing into the cottage but there are so many that they take up every chair, table and a lot of the floor space.

Later, after eating and hearing Santa tell stories, everyone goes outside and rests on candy cane shaped benches and looks around at the North Pole. Santa's eyes light up as he comes up with an idea and says, "Why don't you spend the night and tomorrow, we'll talk about what to do next. Christmas will be coming soon and we'll need to start planning." After saying that, Santa starts counting how many are in the group. When he has gotten everyone counted, he says, "We'll need to divide you all up. Snowdeer, you and your family and Plum Puddin' and Purple Mouse can stay at your cottage. Taper and Tallow, would you please take everyone else over to the Peppermint Suites and make sure they are nice and snug for the night?"

Taper and Tallow both answer, "Yes Sir, Santa," and after everyone thanks Santa and Mrs. Claus and say their goodnights, Taper and Tallow lead them off to the Peppermint Suites. Snowdeer's family, Plum Puddin' and Purple Mouse head to Snowdeer's cottage and go to bed, leaving only Santa and Snowdeer.

Then Santa says, "Snowdeer, I have one more gift for you before I go," and then he walks inside Snowdeer's cottage and returns with a box and hands it to Snowdeer.

Snowdeer opens it, laughs and says, "A Snowdeer wind up alarm clock! Ha! Ha! I love it Santa! Thank you!"

Santa also laughs and kids Snowdeer by saying, "You're the leader of the Team Snowdeer and I want you to always be on time!"

"I will-I promise," replies Snowdeer. So they part ways and Snowdeer stands looking around at Bayberry Bay and at his new North Pole home. He looks up toward the heavens and thanks God for this honor that's been bestowed upon him and then prays a prayer for guidance and help to be the best he can be to spread love, Christmas joy and goodwill.

Then he heads toward his cottage. By now, Tallow and Taper have returned to the cottage entrance and they tell Snowdeer good night and mention that if he needs anything, anytime, to let them know. Snowdeer thanks them and heads through the door. Once inside, he stands there looking over his office and grins at his desk that has SNOWDEER carved in the front. Then his eyes catch a big world map behind his desk. He marvels at how big the world is and how very soon he will be flying around it. He goes into the kitchen and laughs to himself as he relives what Tallow said about them using the table for charting their routes and making sure they don't miss any meals. He then goes to his private lair where he sees his own personal hand carved bed and night stand complete with a bayberry scented candle. He sets his wake up time on his new alarm clock and then puts it on the night stand. His head barely hits his pillow before he drifts off to sleep.

As the alarm goes off the next morning, Snowdeer awakens to the smell of bayberry. He just lays there enjoying the scent and thinks about the wonderful events that have happened in his life and in the lives of his family and friends lately. After a while, he thinks he needs to get up and go wake the gang, but as he looks out the window at Bayberry Bay, he discovers that everyone is already up and skating! "So much for being the leader," he says to himself and then laughs. All of a sudden he hears the doorbell ring and he rushes to the door to find Tasha Mouse and Judy from Dunne's Christmas Buns.

"Good morning Snowdeer. We have some rolls and milk for you," says Tasha.

"And they're freshly baked," Judy says.

"Thank you very much ladies," says Snowdeer. Then Tasha says, "It looks like we'll be seeing a lot of you in the future and we are all very glad you accepted Santa's offer to go around the world. Everyone here at the North Pole is talking about it and wants to know you better!"

"Yes, I'm very glad to be here and I can hardly wait to get to know everyone here too," says Snowdeer.

"I'm looking forward to helping you with toys and clothes to send on your travels," Tasha says. Then she sets the rolls and milk down on a table and says, "I'll have plenty of toys and clothes made for you to pick from down in Santa's secret lair where I do a lot of my work. Please feel free to come down anytime."

Then Judy says, "If you need any rolls Snowdeer, please feel free to come by and pick them up anytime and don't worry about paying 'cause we appreciate you and the work you will be doing here at the North Pole. Please know the door is always open to you."

"Thank You all very much," answers Snowdeer.

Then Judy asks, "Are you planning on skating today on Bayberry Bay Snowdeer?"

Snowdeer answers, "Yes Ma'am, I will later, but for now I'm too excited to leave the cottage! I just want to enjoy your goodies and look around my new place for a while," laughs Snowdeer.

Judy and Tasha laugh with him and Tasha says, "Well, we are going to go Snowdeer. God bless you and please let us know if we can help."

Snowdeer answers, "I sure will, and God bless you all too. Thank you again and see you soon. Bye for now."

20 - GOOD MORNIN', MY LITTLE DEER

After Snowdeer eats his rolls and drinks his milk, he walks over to the window and pulls back the curtain and sees the gang skating on Bayberry Bay. He decides to step outside on the front porch to get a better look at them, but when he opens the door, he finds Taper and Tallow standing guard in front of his cottage door.

They both nod to Snowdeer and Tallow says, "Good morning, Mr. Snowdeer, how are you today?"

Then Taper says, "Is there anything we can do for you Sir?"

"Yes, there is," says Snowdeer. "I would like you to help me find Santa so we can start my training please."

Taper answers, "Mr. Snowdeer, just use the Magical Bell Santa gave you, and he will be right here."

"Oh yeah, I forgot. Thank you Mr. Taper," answers Snowdeer.

"My pleasure, Mr. Snowdeer," replies Taper.

Then Snowdeer says, "I tell you what, let's not worry about using Mr. before our names anymore. You're my friends and we'll be working together for a long time, so let's just go by our first names if you would please."

Taper and Tallow smile and say, "Yes Sir, Snowdeer," and from that time forward, that is just what they would do. Then, Snowdeer goes back inside and walks over to his desk and picks up the Magical Bell and rings it.

Within minutes, Santa comes walking through Snowdeer's cottage door and he says, "HO-HO-HO! Good mornin', my little deer!" Everyone laughs and then Snowdeer looks past Santa and sees Rene Elf and Elva Elf coming through the door.

In unison they say, "Good morning Snowdeer."

Then Rene Elf says, "We heard you ring the bell and we've come to help you."

Snowdeer smiles at them and says. "Thank you very much for coming! I'm ready to fly around the world!"

"Then, HO-HO-HO! On with the show!" says Santa belly laughing. Then Santa starts his training by saying, "Snowdeer, Lesson one is . . . always have fun and do everything with love. If you do everything based on love, your work will never seem like work and you'll make millions of friends and fulfill the dreams and wishes of more people and animals than you could ever imagine."

An excited Snowdeer answers saying, "I will Santa, I promise! What is Lesson Two?"

Santa replies, "Always have plenty of Sugar Snow handy to put on yourself, Rene and Elva Elf, Taper and Tallow, and on whoever is riding in the sleigh with you. Make sure all the deer who will be flying have enough Sugar Snow on them too. You want to be sure you all come back home! HO-HO-HO!" Santa laughs.

Rene Elf also laughs and says, "Yes, I'm in total agreement with you Santa! Me and Elva Elf don't want to have to parachute out of the sleigh if it starts to go down!"

Everyone laughs and then Santa says, "Snowdeer, I'm just kidding you about Lesson Two because the Sugar Snow will always make sure you're covered and kept safe. They have never once let me down, and they never will."

"That's great news Santa! So, what is the real Lesson Two?" asks Snowdeer.

Santa answers, "Lesson Two is to always be prepared. Work closely with Rene, Elva, Taper, Tallow, Plum Puddin', Purple Mouse or whoever is playing a part in making your trip a success. Whoever rides along always needs to know where your next stop will be. Harvey Elf, Russ Elf and Bev Elf will also be going on some of the trips with you so always remember to have everyone watch where you are headed and also to check your special gift list so you know where to deliver the presents."

"Yes Sir Santa!" Snowdeer answers. Then Santa says, "I will need your keen eye to watch through the night and through the day to keep your crew safe and on course. So, with that in mind, I have another gift for you Snowdeer." Then Santa pulls something out of his pocket and says, "This gift I give you has been a secret that only Russ Elf and I knew about. I asked Russ Elf to build this Magical Compass that will give perfect direction so you won't miss any of the places you are headed to.

Also, you didn't know this, but Taper and Tallow have magical candle wicks inside them and when Sugar Snow is put on them, they light up and will not burn out for the whole trip! They will help light your way so the lists can be read perfectly, and you can see where you are going."

"Wow Santa, you thought of everything," says Snowdeer.

"I try," replies Santa laughing.

Then Snowdeer asks, "Is there a Lesson three sir?"

Santa answers, "Yes, there is Snowdeer. But first, we need to go get your sleigh and place it on the take-off pad for you to learn this lesson. Then, we'll have Harvey Elf harness your family of deer to your sleigh. After they are harnessed, we'll have Gary and Jennie Elf load your sleigh and Russ Elf will bring along something else he made. A Magical Musical Box that will play Christmas music during your trips. If you should happen to fly out at Easter time, Russ Elf can even make it play Easter music. If you fly out during Thanksgiving, Russ can have it play songs of Thanks to the Lord so, whatever music you want to hear, for whatever season you are in, Russ can put it on your Magical Music Box while you are flying."

Snowdeer says, "That is wonderful! Thank you Santa! But for me, I could listen to Christmas music on every flight 'cause, I'm always having Christmas on the inside", and then he laughs.

"HO-HO-HO! That's the Spirit," says Santa laughing and then he asks, "Well, is everyone ready to begin our first take off practice?"

"Yes Sir Santa-we're ready," they all reply.

"Ok, let's get everything together," says Santa. Then he starts instructing the gang saying, "Rene and Elva Elf, please go and get an old Christmas List so we can pretend we're out delivering gifts. Taper and Tallow, please go get Russ Elf and have him put Snowdeer's favorite Christmas music in the Magical Music Box. And then, after the Sugar Snow has arrived, Taper and Tallow, please light yourselves with Sugar Snow and then stand in Snowdeer's sleigh on each side of Snowdeer. I'll go get Jennie, Gary and Harvey Elf and have them bring over Snowdeer's sleigh to get it ready for take-off. Then, I'll have Jennie Elf go to the North Pole's pole and ask the Sugar Snow to fly over to help us. I'll go find Bev Elf to round up the rest of the gang and after the deer have arrived, I'll have Gary and Harvey Elf harness them up to the sleigh. And last, but not least, Snowdeer, I want you to go with me so that we can be sure we'll make sure everything is done when we get to the take-off pad. Then, we'll be prepared to fly."

"That sounds great Santa," says Snowdeer.

"Then, HO-HO-HO! Let's all prepare to go!" says Santa. Then off they all go to do their duty in making Snowdeer's first day one to remember.

21 - SNOWDEER'S TRIAL RUN
TO DOE RUN AND BRANSON

After everyone arrives at the sleigh take-off pad, Santa asks to have the deer harnessed to the sleigh. When that's done, they stand silently on the pad waiting for Santa's next orders. Santa looks at each one and smiles and says, "What a great day! I'm so proud of you all! HO-HO-HO!" Then looking at Bev Elf he asks, "Bev Elf, would you please say a prayer for us and then we'll be on our way."

After Bev Elf says a beautiful prayer for protection and to be a blessing, Santa and an excited team of people and deer await Santa's next command. Then Santa says, "Everyone get in your places! For our trial run, we will head to Doe Run down in the Ozarks! Does that place sound familiar Snowdeer?"

"Yes Sir!" an excited Snowdeer answers.

Then Santa takes a deep breath and shouts, "SUGAR SNOW! SUGAR SNOW! ON SNOWDEER'S SLEIGH AND TEAM PLEASE BLOW!" In a matter of seconds, a big wind starts blowing and the Sugar Snow comes flying and swirling and circling every one of the gang! They watch as these magical white Sugar Snowflakes laugh and light up and even blow on some of the gang, tickling them! Sugar Snow circles Taper and Tallow and causes their wicks to light up with flames that are very bright. "My, my, Sugar Snow, you are in rare form today! You are as excited to see this trip happen as I am," says Santa. After he says that, the Sugar Snow laughs and gangs up on Santa circling him and tickling him and causing him to bust out in laughter, giving a continuous, HO-HO-HO!

After they stop and Santa gets his composure, he gasps as he looks around and sees that the people of the North Pole Village have gathered to watch this event! "I guess my voice carries more than I thought! HO-HO-HO!" says Santa. Then Santa looks over and sees Mrs. Claus watching and he invites her to come over to stand by him. Seeing that they have created a crowd, Santa laughs and says, "Welcome Everyone to Snowdeer's first practice run! Today marks the first of many trips around the world he will be making!" Santa turns around and sees the Snowdeer family. Jim-Buck, Deerlores, Deerell, Rosie, Antler, Longnose, Ken-Buck & Mark-Buck-all eagerly waiting with Plum Puddin', Purple Mouse, Carrot, Branson the Balladeer, Dosi Doe, Bev Elf, Darrell and Rose Marie, mounted on each of the reindeer. Then Santa shouts, "SUGAR SNOW! SUGAR SNOW! OFF TO DOE RUN WE GO!" At this command, the Sugar Snow, who had moved up and over to the side of the gang, immediately blows down and circles them once again, and then makes them take off in a big rush, and off they go toward Doe Run. The crowd cheers wildly as they feel the breezy chilly wind from the Sugar Snows mighty take off! Santa says, "HO-HO-HO! They left us in the cold!" which makes the crowd laugh. While Santa is laughing, Mrs. Claus tip toes up to him and gives him a kiss on the cheek. The crowd goes, "Ah" and Santa says, "That's my girl, Mrs. Claus!" and then he puts his arm around her and they all return to watching Snowdeer's sleigh and the team of deer as the Sugar Snow quickly takes them to Doe Run.

After the sleigh is no longer in sight, Santa laughs and says, "This is cause for celebration! Everyone go by Krull's Confectionary where I will personally serve you hot cocoa! Mrs. Claus, would you go over to Marquart's Molasses and serve hot cocoa there please dear? We have a big crowd and we need both places to serve cocoa."

"Why sure Santa," answers Mrs. Claus.

Then Santa continues, "And because I want to make sure we have enough for everyone, I want to have cocoa served at Plummer's Reindeer Hardware too. They not only have great guest service, but they make a great cup of hot cocoa for their guests too! Believe me, I have tasted the hot cocoa at every business here at the North Pole and I'm an authority on it!" says Santa laughing. "The only place that doesn't serve hot cocoa is Body by Dorn. He told me that Mewlinda the cat drank all the milk and he can't keep it in stock. Do you think that is true?"

"Why sure dear," Mrs. Claus answers and winks at the crowd.

"Well, let's get going and get these folks something to drink," says Santa. So off they go to get the hot cocoa ready to serve to the North Pole villagers.

Later, while on the way back to their cottage, Santa says to Mrs. Claus, "You know, as much fun as Snowdeer and the gang were having, it's hard tellin' when they'll be back!"

"Yes, you're right about that dear. I hope Rene and Elva Elf brought along a picnic lunch for everyone.

And that Plum Puddin' took along some plum pudding!" says Mrs. Claus joking.

Santa laughs and as they arrive at the cottage door, Mrs. Claus says, "Dear, you ought to go take a nap. They're going to need you a whole lot when they get back."

Santa replies, "That sounds like a great idea Mrs. Claus. I'll go and do that. Wake me up when they arrive please." Then he jokingly says, "As in the words of Harvey the Elf, "HA-HA-HA, HO-HO-HO! IT'S OFF TO THE BUNKHOUSE BUNK I GO!" They both laugh and Santa walks over to his big soft recliner, takes off his coat and kicks off his boots and lays back. Within about 2 minutes, he's snoring.

Mrs. Claus laughs to herself and goes to the closet to get a patchwork quilt that Terrie Young Deer had sewn just for them and that Plum Puddin' had delivered to them some Christmases ago. She places it across Santa and then leaves him to nap while she goes to visit Josh, Amber, Lilly Kay Elf and Ilsa Marie Elf down the road.

Meanwhile, Snowdeer and the gang are having the time of their life! In the sleigh, Taper and Tallow are fully lit and hoping the wind doesn't blow out their candlelight. Rene Elf looks at them and reminds them saying, "Your lights will never go out because the Sugar Snow magic dust will keep you lit. So even on the windiest days or nights, you will remain burning."

"Thank you for the reminder Miss Rene, we appreciate that," they answer.

"How about some music?" asks Russ Elf.

"Yes!" they all answer back, so Russ Elf puts his Magical Music Box up where a bag of presents would normally be sitting and starts turning the crank. Out comes some of the most beautiful Christmas music and everyone's excitement gets even greater!

The Sugar Snow whisper to each other and some of them go up to Russ Elf and say something to him. He nods to them and then turns the crank a little bit more and stops. All of a sudden the Sugar Snow goes into a snow flake show! They circle everyone over and over and tickle some of them and laugh. Even though it isn't night yet, they light up in a bright white and then change into boldly colored lights. All the gang cheers at the sight and for at least 20 minutes they put on a spectacular light show. After they've finished, they go back to flying along with the sleigh.

Just after they'd settled down, they all hear Snowdeer shout, "The Doe Run Forest is approaching!"

Everyone cheers and Rene Elf says, "Now, if this were a regular stop, we would check our list to see who we are to deliver gifts to. Then Snowdeer, you or whoever you choose, would deliver the gifts. But, if you are on an a diplomatic trip as an ambassador to spread good will and not deliver gifts, you would just go to the door and knock and speak with them personally."

Then Snowdeer says, "Wow, I can hardly wait 'till we're doing it for real! When do you think we can start?"

Rene replies, "I don't know for sure Snowdeer, but now that it's getting closer to Christmas, I bet Santa will have you off and running within a week or so."

"That soon?" asks Snowdeer.

Rene answers, "Yes, I believe Santa will, because he needs you to go out into the world and bring Christmas cheer all the time. Anytime of the year. The truth is Snowdeer, people and animals need the joy that Christmas brings. The joy that is found through Jesus. The source of all joy. He is the One we celebrate at Christmas. We don't actually know the date when Jesus was born, but December 25th is when we celebrate His birth. He was born in a small village called Bethlehem in Israel. He was a great man. But more importantly, was the Son of God. He came to live a perfect life and then died on a cross at Calvary, in Jerusalem (that's in Israel too) for the sins of mankind, so that whoever accepts Him as their Savior would go to Heaven when they die."

"What a great Man," says Snowdeer.

Rene shakes her head yes and then continues, "Yes, that's for sure and there is much more to His story Snowdeer. After Jesus was crucified, He was buried but then rose from the grave and later ascended to Heaven and He is there now!"

"Wow, that story keeps getting better and better! Rene, will we get to go to Bethlehem or Jerusalem on any of our trips?" asks Snowdeer.

Rene answers, "Yes, I'm sure we will go to both places." "Santa always stops at both and I am certain you will too."

"That is wonderful. I really want to go there," says Snowdeer.

"We want to go there too," the rest of the gang chime in.

"I'm positive we will," answers Rene.

"I want to do that too, but I guess In the meantime, we'll have to only pretend we're on a delivery trip there," says Elva Elf. "Tell you what, I'll read off a name and we'll play like we're going to someone's house to deliver a present. Let's land in a field instead of on the roof of a home because we don't want them to see or hear us, and then we can practice taking off again."

So, Elva and Rene Elf would read a name off and they would practice landing in a field. Then Snowdeer, Russ Elf or whoever wanted, would play like they were delivering presents by jumping out of the sleigh and acting like they were sliding down a chimney and then come back to the sleigh and then jump back on. Rene, Elva or Harvey the Elf would make a check mark beside the name and what gift was given and what town they were in. Then Snowdeer would give a command for Sugar Snow to circle them and magically cause them to fly off again. They did this for several hours and eventually it started to get dark.

Plum Puddin' looks down and sees that they are flying toward Jim-Buck, Deerlores and Snowdeer's cabin and he lets them know. Deerlores says if they would like to stop, she would feed everyone and they could relax for a little while. They take her up on her offer and have a nice meal.

As they are getting harnessed up again and preparing for take-off, Branson the Balladeer asks, "Can we go to Branson to see my daddy Reuben and my mama Mary Branson please?"

Snowdeer lights up at the idea and says, "Why yes, we sure can." So Snowdeer gives the command for the Sugar Snow to take them to Reuben and Mary Branson's cabin at the little country community of Branson that was named after them. In a little bit, they arrive and Branson the Balladeer and his sister Dosi Doe jump off the sleigh and run to the cabin.

They knock on the door and listen as they hear a man's voice inside saying, "It's late, I wonder who that'd be?"

Then they hear a woman's voice saying, "I don't know. Make sure you got your shotgun handy in case there's any trouble." Branson the Balladeer and Dosi Doe hear Reuben and Mary's footsteps and then watch as the cabin door opens. There Reuben Branson stands, holding a lantern with Mary standing right behind him. When they see that it is Dosi Doe and Branson the Balladeer, he just about drops his lantern and Mary hollers! With tears in his eyes, Reuben grabs Branson in a big ole hug and says, "Son, we were so worried about you."

Branson the Balladeer answers him back, "Daddy, I am so sorry. I had a horrible time in that snowstorm, but Santa found me and took great care of me. I had lost my memory for a while, but I got better and started singin' and writin' songs again."

Mary comes out from behind Reuben and hugs him and with tears in her eyes she says, "Branson, I am so thankful you were found! I have prayed so much that we would see ya again."

Then Reuben says, "Son, we named this town after us, but without having you here, it was never the same. Now, it can be the way we always wanted it to be with our family back together."

Branson says to him, "Yes, Daddy, but I want to tell you that I also have a home at the North Pole and will be going back and forth to both places." Then, he tells Reuben and Mary what he does at the North Pole and how Santa is counting on him to help. He wants to assure them that he will always be coming back to stay with them and to help take care of them.

Reuben says, "We understand. We love you and want you to be happy."

Mary says, "Now that we have seen you again and know that you are alive and safe, you do whatever you want. We are always here for you Son. Don't ya ever forget that."

Branson the Balladeer says, "Thank you Mama and Daddy, I will never forget it. I love you all so much and I will be back soon. That's a promise!"

Reuben and Mary then look at Dosi Doe and Reuben says, "We want you to know that we love you too Dosi Doe, and if you decide to live at both Branson and the North Pole like your brother is doing, we understand.

Then Mary breaks in and says, "Just bring us a gift from Santa every Christmas," and they all laugh.

Dosi Doe hugs her folks and says, "Thank you Daddy and Mama for understanding. I do plan on living at both places and I want you to meet Santa. He is so nice and I will try to see that y'all meet."

"We would love that Dosi Doe," says Mary.

Then Dosi Doe tells her Mama and Daddy about Snowdeer's new duty of flying around the world delivering gifts and being an ambassador of good will for Santa. She tells them that she is excited to be a part of that good will team along with Branson the Balladeer.

Reuben and Mary get so excited and Reuben asks Snowdeer, "You reckon me and the Mrs. could ride along with you all sometime?"

Snowdeer answers, "Yes Sir, Mr. Branson, I know Santa wouldn't mind at all. We can have you ride at the same time as Dosi Doe and Branson the Balladeer so you can go as a family and Branson can sing for all of us!"

"Then that's what we'll do Snowdeer," says Reuben.

Then Mary says, "Thank You, Mr. Snowdeer. You all come back and I'll fix you all a big ole country meal!"

"Thank you Mrs. Branson, I will definitely take you up on that offer," says Snowdeer.

"Y'all wanna go over and see Grandpa Jack and Nana Sherry?" asks Reuben.

"Are they up?" asks Branson the Balladeer.

"Yes, I can see their cabin from here and it's lit up. They had a Bible study tonight and a big feed too! You know how those good ole Presbyterians are!" says Reuben and then he laughs.

"Oh yeah, I understand 'cause I used to be in that Bible study. Nana Sherry knows how to cook and Grandpa Jack and I used to go explorin' in the caves," says Branson the Balladeer.

"Well, why don't you go over to their cabin and pay 'em a visit?" asks Mary.

"Yes, I'd love to Mama," answers Branson.

So, Branson the Balladeer, Dosi Doe, Snowdeer and Plum Puddin' head over to Grandpa Jacks and Nana Sherry's. Branson the Balladeer knocks on their door and Grandpa Jack answers the door holding a lantern with their dog Lickerish standing at his side and he says, "Welcome back Branson The Balladeer and Dosi Doe! How are y'all? We were so worried about you! Come on in! Then he looks at Snowdeer and Plum Puddin' and asks, "Who are your friends?"

Nana Sherry, who had been straightening up the cabin after their meal and Bible study, walks up to them and says, "Well, if it isn't Branson The Balladeer & Dosi Doe! Welcome! We're so glad Y'all are alright! We've been praying for you! Please, sit down for a while and tell us what you've been doing!"

Then Dosi Doe and Branson the Balladeer hug them both and Branson says, "Hello! It's wonderful to see you all again! I have sure missed you!" Then Branson introduces them to Snowdeer and Plum Puddin' and then he tells them Snowdeer's story about his Christmas Wish to pull Santa's sleigh one Christmas and how Santa granted his wish, so he delivered gifts all around the world. Branson also tells them that by request from Santa himself, Snowdeer is going to be flying around the world delivering gifts and being an ambassador of good will all the time. Branson the Balladeer then tells them his own story about how he was stuck in a snowstorm and how he almost died and how Santa picked him up in the woods and took him back to live at the North Pole. He also tells them how Snowdeer, Dosi Doe and himself are going to live part time at the North Pole and part time in the Ozarks.

Grandpa Jack and Nana Sherry get excited about their stories and Snowdeer gets an idea and asks them, "Would y'all like to go on a trip sometime to the North Pole with us?"

With great excitement they both say, "Yes! We'd love to go!"

"Then it is decided. We will be taking you on a trip very soon," says Snowdeer.

"We look forward to it," says Grandpa Jack and then Nana Sherry says, "The North Pole is the second place I'd love to go to. The Holy Land is the first place I want to travel to and I hope to go there someday."

Then Snowdeer says, "I'm planning on flying there sometime during my travels and I will come by to pick you up on the way over."

"We would love that very much. Thank you," says Sherry.

"Speakin' of the North Pole, we'd better get going and get back up there before Santa wonders what happened to us," laughs Snowdeer.

"Ok" Branson the Balladeer and Dosi Doe say, and so they give Grandpa Jack and Nana Sherry a hug before they leave. Snowdeer and Plum Puddin' watch with great admiration, the love between them.

Then Sherry looks at Snowdeer and Plum Puddin' and says, "Get over here and give me a hug too! We consider you part of the family now. Anyone who knows Santa and can drive a sleigh around the world deserves a good hug!" They all laugh and Snowdeer and Plum Puddin' happily oblige Sherry's wishes.

Then, Branson the Balladeer asks them, "You wanna watch us take off to the North Pole in Snowdeer's sleigh?"

They both say yes, so they all head over to Reuben and Mary's cabin to watch Snowdeer and all take off. Reuben and Mary welcome Grandpa Jack and Nana Sherry and Snowdeer introduces everyone to them. The excitement grows as everyone watches Snowdeer and Plum Puddin' get the deer harnessed up and in their places. The excitement grows even more as they see the Sugar Snow rise off the ground and up into the air waiting for its orders.

Then Snowdeer says, "Everyone say these magic words together, "SUGAR SNOW! SUGAR SNOW! BACK TO THE NORTH POLE WE GO!" The Sugar Snow flies up and then drops down and swirls over all of them. Then, the sleigh and all of the gang rise up in the air and as they wave goodbye, the Sugar Snow causes them to take off in a rush and swiftly head toward to the North Pole. Bev Elf hollers back to Russ Elf to crank up the Magical Music Box so it will play Christmas music, so he starts to crank it and beautiful Christmas music once again flies through the air with them giving them a great feeling of Christmas. Snowdeer gets a big grin on his face and he hollers up to his Mama and Daddy-Jim-Buck and Deerlores-asking, "Are y'all having a great time up there?"

"Yes, we are Son!" they both holler back.

"Thanks to you and Santa, we are having the time of our lives," says Jim-Buck.

"We will go with you as often as you want us to," says Deerlores.

"Well, Mama and Daddy, in that case, you will be going all the time," answers Snowdeer laughing.

They all fly through the night sky admiring the beautiful stars when Rene Elf gets an idea and leans over to Snowdeer and asks, "Do you think the Sugar Snow would put us on a light show tonight?"

Snowdeer answers her saying, "Great idea Rene!" Then he looks around at the Sugar Snow and asks them, "Sugar Snow, would you put us on a special light show tonight please?"

One of the Sugar Snow flakes comes up to Snowdeer and answers him saying, "Yes, we would be happy to."

Then another Sugar Snow flake flies up to Snowdeer and says, "My pleasure-count me in!" Then one after another, they fly up to Snowdeer and tell him they would do a show anytime he wants and how they appreciate being a part of the team.

Plum Puddin's mama Rose Marie looks up while riding one of the deer and she asks the Sugar Snow, "Can y'all sing too?"

Some of the Sugar Snow rush over to her and tell her, "Yes, we can. Would you like to hear us?"

"Yes, please do," answers Rose Marie.

"Will you turn different colors too?" asks Plum Puddin's daddy Darrell.

"Yes, we sure will," one of the Sugar Snow answers.

"We may have to take this act on the road someday," Darrell says to Rose Marie.

"Yes, you sing and play guitar and I'll sing and play accordion and Plum Puddin'-you sing and play doghouse bass while the Sugar Snow lights up the stage!"

"Ok, Mama, let's do it!" answers Plum Puddin'.

Snowdeer's brothers Longnose, Antler, Deerell and sister Rosie along with Jim-Buck, Deerlores, Ken-Buck and Mark-Buck start cheering saying, "Sugar Snow! Sugar Snow! Sugar Snow! Sugar Snow!..."

So Snowdeer leans back and with a loud voice says, "SUGAR SNOW! SUGAR SNOW! SING FOR US AND LIGHT YOUR SNOW!" and with that, the Sugar Snow get together in a big huddle and you can hear little voices whispering. Then all of a sudden, they turn a beautiful bright white and come flying down and circle every one of the gang and the sleigh. Russ Elf knows they are up to something great, so he turns the Magical Music Box off. After he does that, the Sugar Snow stops in mid-air! Then they burst forth in song and start changing colors and start making shapes of Santa, Mrs. Claus, Snowdeer and everyone who is traveling on this trip! The Sugar Snow circles them again causing the sleigh and the deer to stop in the air without the need to fly! The gang can hardly take it all in as they watch the Sugar Snow perform the most beautiful songs and light show that any of them had ever seen! Purple Mouse blushes his purple color when he sees the Sugar Snow make a shape like him and a shape like Tasha Mouse and then have her lean over give him a kiss on the cheek. Everyone turns and looks at a very purple Purple Mouse and he just shakes his head, but secretly he's enjoying it. The Sugar Snow go into their own original song, "A Sugar Snow Christmas," and they spell it in the sky. They spell it in white but then change colors in the words. At the end of their last song they form a shape like a big waterfall and come down it in different shades of blue and then they go crazy making a variety of colors while shooting across the sky. Then, they swirl around everyone again and after doing this, the deer and sleigh start flying again. The Sugar Snow then flies ahead of them forming a huge Christmas tree with white lights and then turn into colored lights and then they turn into the word, North Pole with a bright candy cane colored arrow that's pointing them north. The whole gang cheers and goes full speed ahead while Russ Elf turns the Magical Music Box back on. What a wonderful night the gang have as they travel on Snowdeer's trial run to Doe Run and Branson.

22 - SNOWDEER AND THE SNOWMOON

As Snowdeer and the gang are getting closer to the North Pole, they see the glow of the Village. The gangs excitement builds and some of the Sugar Snow flakes fly on ahead to let Santa and the North Pole Village know they are on their way. The Sugar Snow flies over to Strike the Bell to let him know they are back so he can ring his bell to let everyone in the village know the gang is coming. Then they fly over to the Claus' cottage and blow at the front door. No one answers, so the Sugar Snow go to a nearby window and peek in. Mrs. Claus is still gone visiting at Josh, Amber, Lilly Kay and Ilsa Marie Elf's cottage and Santa is sound asleep in his high top chair reclined back and covered up in a patchwork quilt snoring. The Sugar Snow laugh and giggle at the sight and then huddle together to try to think of a way to wake up Santa. They decide to do just what Santa would do. Go down the chimney! They check first to see if Santa has a fire going in the fireplace. But after the many hours Mrs. Santa had been gone, and with Santa taking a long nap, the fire had gone out. So, with more laughing and giggling, the Sugar Snow fly up and over the cottage and start going down the chimney.

Once inside, they fly over to Santa who is right beside the fireplace and one of them touch his nose. Santa wiggles it a little bit then some of the other Sugar Snow touch his ears. Santa jerks his head and some more of them go to his feet and start tickling his toes. Once again, Santa jerks but now realizes he has company. Then he says, "Ho-Ho-Ho! I see we have an indoor snowstorm!" They all laugh and Santa says, "Did everyone else make it back from Doe Run?"

One of the Sugar Snow says, "Yes Santa, and they will be here in just a few minutes."

Then Santa says, "HO-HO-HO! Let's go tell Strike the Bell so he can ring them in!"

As Santa puts on his boots and grabs his coat to go outside, one of the Sugar Snow says, "Santa Sir, we already let him know."

Santa smiles and says, "Great job Sugar Snow. Now, let's go to the landing pad and watch them fly in!" So, as they start walking toward the landing pad, they hear Strike starting to ring. People from all over the village rush out of their homes and Santa announces, "Snowdeer and his gang are on their way! Let's head over to the landing pad to welcome them home!" The crowd cheers and then they hear in the distance Christmas music playing. As they look up, they see a large happy group of travelers being led in by the bright Sugar Snow! The villagers dash over to the landing pad and watch the Sugar Snow circle around the pad and then light up the landing strip so Snowdeer and the team can see clearly to land.

Strike keeps ringing as they arrive and as the deer and sleigh touch ground, the villagers cheer wildly! Mrs. Claus, Josh, Amber, Lilly Kay and Ilsa Marie Elf had rushed over just in time to see the landing. Santa sees them and walks over and gives Mrs. Claus a kiss on the cheek and then looks at Josh Elf and asks, "Josh, would you sing a song please?"

Josh answer, "Yes, Sir Santa, my pleasure." So Josh gets out his guitar and walks up to the front by Snowdeer and the sleigh and begins singing Joy To The World. Amber, Lilly Kay and Ilsa Marie Elf join him and Santa invites everyone to sing along.

The whole village sounds wonderful and when Josh finishes, Santa says, "Everyone, please join us over at Bayberry Bay where we will have a skating party with hot cocoa and cookies and then take a tour of Snowdeer's new headquarters! HO-HO-HO!"

Then Harvey Elf runs up to Santa and whispers in his ear. Santa laughs and then announces, "By special request of Harvey, we will be having a light show brought to you by Sugar Snow! Everyone cheers and then Santa looks to the sky where the Sugar Snow is flying around waiting for the order to start the show. Then, with a loud voice, Santa says to the Sugar Snow, "SUGAR SNOW! SUGAR SNOW! PUT ON A GREAT LIGHT SHOW!" and the Sugar Snow immediately bursts through the air and flies over to Bayberry Bay circling the whole bay with their beautiful light!

They start with a solid white light and then go into all being the same color and then to turning different colors. They dash through the sky making the shapes of Santa, Mrs. Santa, Snowdeer, Plum Puddin', Purple Mouse and everyone who went on that first trip! They also make the shapes of candy canes, snowmen and reindeer. The crowd gasps as they see the Sugar Snow give them the best light show they've ever seen! Russ and Bev Elf bring over the Magical Music Box and Russ starts to play it. The Sugar Snow flies down and circles the villagers and puts everyone into a great Christmas mood!

Snowdeer says to Plum Puddin', "I wish I could fly like that!"

Plum Puddin' answers saying, "You can Snowdeer! Just ask the Sugar Snow to coat you with their magic dust and you can fly along with them!"

Snowdeer says, "I wanna do it!"

So, Plum Puddin' goes over to some of the Sugar Snow and talks with them. Some of them immediately fly over to Snowdeer and let him know they would be happy to help him fly. Snowdeer tells them, "Yes, please help me. I want to fly with you."

Then the Sugar Snow laughs and say OK, and then they start swirling around him. The next thing Snowdeer knows, he's flying up and around the crowd! Snowdeer laughs uncontrollably and when he looks down at the North Pole village, he sees that his friends have gathered and everyone is watching him fly!

While Rose Marie is looking up at Snowdeer, she notices the moon behind him and says to Darrell, "Look! There's a Snow Moon up above Snowdeer! It's white like he is!"

Others hear what Rose Marie said and within minutes, everyone is looking at the big bright Snow Moon above Snowdeer. All of a sudden, Snowdeer flies to a place in the sky where the moon is completely behind him and is circled around him! He's like a picture in a big round frame! All who are watching below gasp as they see the beautiful light of the Snow Moon behind Snowdeer!

They all cheer for Snowdeer and as he flies past the moon, Deerlores gets a shocked look on her face and she says to Jim-Buck, "Look at the moon! Am I dreaming or is that Snowdeer's image in the moon?" Others overhear what Deerlores said and they begin to look up and they too see Snowdeer's image in the moon.

"Yes, I believe it is him Deerlores," answers Jim-Buck. "Now, when we're back home in Doe Run, we'll be able to see our son whether he's with us or in the Snow Moon!"

Deerlores agrees and says, "That's right Jim-Buck. We will always be able to see him and remember him."

By now, the whole crowd has seen the Snowdeer Snow Moon and they start cheering. Snowdeer hears them and he decides to come down to see what they are cheering about. After he lands, he walks up to Jim-Buck and Deerlores. Deerlores says, "Snowdeer, we saw something amazing while you were flying. After you flew past the Snow Moon, we discovered your image on it!"

Snowdeer says, "Really Momma?" Then Jim-Buck says,

"Yes, Snowdeer, just look up and you can see yourself." So, when Snowdeer looks up at the moon, he gasps and stares in unbelief. The moon did indeed have an image of him in it!

"I can't believe it!" Snowdeer says while still staring at the moon. He runs over to Santa and says, "Santa! Did you see that?"

Santa replies, "Yes Snowdeer, It's a special Snow Moon for a special Snowdeer! I believe this is your night, MY LITTLE DEER! HO-HO-HO!"

They all laugh and Snowdeer turns back to look at the moon. The rest of the night everyone skates and drinks hot cocoa, eats cookies and tours Snowdeer's new headquarters. After a while, the crowd starts going home leaving Santa and Snowdeer by themselves.

Snowdeer asks Santa, "When do we go out again?"

Santa answers, "Let's go down to my secret lair and we'll talk about it."

So, they walk over to the reindeer barn to the door that leads down the great staircase to Santa's lair. As Santa and Snowdeer go down the staircase and walk by great displays of pictures through the years; treasure chests of gold and silver coins and toy after toy, Snowdeer is once again reminded of the legend he is now associated with. He is humbled by all of this.

Santa knows what he is thinking and he says, "Snowdeer, always remember. Your mission is to bring joy and happiness to all the people and animals of the world. Don't get distracted by the riches. As long as you remember that, you will always be rich."

Snowdeer answers, "Thank you Santa, I will always remember that."

Then Santa says, "I know you will Snowdeer because I know your heart and that's why I chose you. Not everyone could do the job you've been chosen to do."

Snowdeer says, "Santa, it's an honor and I'll never let you down."

Santa smiles and takes Snowdeer through his whole underground lair showing him everything and teaching him to be a great ambassador of love, kindness, peace and goodwill to all men and animals. They talk into the night and Snowdeer grows by leaps and bounds in knowledge and wisdom. He now understands that this is what he is meant to do.

As they walk up the stairs and leave the underground lair and go outside, Santa says, "Snowdeer, we need to send everyone back home tomorrow except you, Plum Puddin' and Purple Mouse. I want to teach them some things that will help make your travels easier. You'll find no better friends than those two and they really want to help you." Then Santa yawns and says, "Snowdeer, my buddy, we'd better go to bed. We have a lot to do tomorrow."

"Yes Sir Santa," replies Snowdeer and off Santa goes to his cottage leaving Snowdeer alone. Snowdeer looks up at the Snow Moon and grins real big as he sees himself in it. Then he walks up to his headquarters and sees Taper and Tallow asleep by the front doors. He tippy toes past them and once inside, he lights a lantern and looks around his new place. He wonders how he ever got this far with his life. And how many adventures lie ahead for him as he travels around the world with his friends? Then he says a prayer thanking God for blessing him and asking for guidance. Eventually, he starts feeling very tired and decides to go to bed. He winds up the clock Santa gave him, blows out the lantern, gets under the covers and goes right to sleep.

23 - BACK TO THE OZARK MOUNTAINS

The next morning, Snowdeer, Plum Puddin' and Purple Mouse meet with the gang at Snowdeer's headquarters. Santa and Mrs. Claus are there and Santa says, "Welcome everybody! It's been a great pleasure having each and every one of you visit us! Mrs. Claus and I want to thank you all for coming and seeing how life is here at the North Pole. We are very sad to see so many of you going back, but you have an open invitation to come visit anytime." Then he says while chuckling, "You know a few friends who have magical jars who can bring you here!" Everyone laughs and Santa continues, "Snowdeer, Plum Puddin' and Purple Mouse will be staying here to undergo more training. They'll be going out soon to do a pre-Christmas trip to get folks around the world in the Christmas Spirit and to get some of the Naughty ones back on the Nice List! HO-HO-HO!"

Once again, everyone laughs and Plum Puddin' says, "Well everybody, I reckon it's time for the Sugar Snow to take you south, back to the Ozark Mountains!"

So they all say their goodbyes and Santa says to them, "Everyone, gather in a circle and I'm going to ask the Sugar Snow to take you home." Then he turns to the Sugar Snow and asks them, "Would you please take them home, Sugar Snow?"

The Sugar Snow flies up in the air and starts sparkling and lighting up in a brilliant white and some go up to Santa and swirl around him saying, "Yes, we will be happy to Santa!"

Then Santa says, "Thank you Sugar Snow". He then turns around to the gang and says, "SUGAR SNOW! SUGAR SNOW! BACK TO THE OZARK MOUNTAINS GO!"

The Sugar Snow starts flying up and swirling around the gang and in an instant, they are gone! Plum Puddin', Snowdeer and Purple Mouse look at each other and then at Santa.

Plum Puddin' says, "Santa, we're here to help you anyway we can."

Purple Mouse nods his head in agreement and asks, "Santa, what would you have us do?"

Santa and Mrs. Claus smile back at him and Santa says, "Purple Mouse, I have many things I want you to do with Snowdeer and Plum Puddin', but one of the main things I want is for you and Plum Puddin' to go pick up Pine Cone Chips on a regular basis so we will always have treats to send along for the people you will be flying to meet."

"I'll be happy to do that Santa," says Purple Mouse.

"I will too Santa," says Plum Puddin'.

Then Santa gets a big grin on his face and says, "Well, North Pole Kingdom Flyers, are you ready for more training?" "Yes Sir, we sure are," they answer. "Ok, let's head over to my underground headquarters and Tasha will have your list waiting."

24 - BRANSON

When they reach the last step of the big staircase in Santa's underground headquarters, Tasha Mouse is there to meet them with a long list and a big platter of chocolate chip cookies and milk. They thank her and as Tasha and Purple Mouse's eyes meet, he immediately blushes in a bright purple! Not being able to control it, he looks down and then looks at Snowdeer and Plum Puddin' and whispers, "Oops." They all laugh and Tasha walks off grinning.

Santa puts a cookie in his mouth and then picks up the big platter and walks over and sets it on his desk and says, "We're gonna need this 'cause we're gonna be here awhile! HO-HO-HO!"

Then he shows Snowdeer, Plum Puddin' and Purple Mouse the list of things they need to know to become great ambassadors of peace and goodwill. He then takes them around and shows them all of the toys, games, clothing, and everything else that either he or they will be taking on future trips. They are so fascinated by all of these gifts that they can hardly wait to go out to deliver them!

Snowdeer looks at Santa and asks, "Where do we go next?"

"Branson," answers Santa.

"Branson?" questions Snowdeer.

"Yes, because before he left today, Ken-Buck took me aside and let me know that he is moving his Pine Cone Chip factory over by Lake Taneycomo there in Branson and that very shortly he will be ready to make as many Pine Cone Chips as we need," says Santa.

Snowdeer is thrilled and he says, "That's wonderful news Santa!" Then Snowdeer remembers that Branson is Branson the Balladeer's home place and he says, "We gotta go tell Branson the Balladeer! He'll be so excited that Pine Cone Chips is moving to where his folks live! Reuben, Mary, Dosi Doe, Grandpa Jack and Nana Sherry will be so excited too! Can we take Branson the Balladeer with us when we go there to pick up the Pine Cone Chips?"

"Yes, you sure can take him, and he can go as many times as he wants. We'll put him to work loading and unloading the Pine Cone Chips," laughs Santa. "I can hardly wait to tell him!" says Snowdeer.

Then Santa says, "There's another surprise, but you have to wait 'till you see your Uncle Ken-Buck, so he can tell you. And I can guarantee, it's great!"

Snowdeer sighs and says, "You're gonna make us wait?"

Santa answers, "Yes, I'm really sorry. They made me promise not to tell and Santa is a man who keeps his promises. How I would love to be the one to tell you though!"

Then Plum Puddin' gets an idea and asks, "Santa, could we please go to Uncle Ken-Bucks today and help him move to Branson?"

Purple Mouse grins and says, "Yeah, and we can find out the secret they won't let you tell us Santa."

Santa gives a big, "HO-HO-HO!" and says, "Sure, you can go today, but before you go, Mrs. Claus will prepare you all a meal. So let's head over to the cottage and eat and then you can be on your way."

"Thank you Santa, you are sure full of surprises," says Purple Mouse and they all laugh. Snowdeer and Plum Puddin' nod in agreement and they start walking over to Santa's cottage for a meal.

After they've finished eating, Santa pats his belly and thanks Mrs. Claus for the great meal and gives her a kiss on the cheek. Snowdeer, Plum Puddin' and Purple Mouse also thank her.

As they turn to leave, Mrs. Claus says, "You boys have a safe trip and tell all of the gang down there I said hello and for them to come back here to visit us soon."

As they are leaving the cottage, Snowdeer asks Santa, "Who's gonna fly the sleigh today? All of my family are back in the Ozarks."

Santa answers, "Snowdeer, this trip is going to be a lot different. We're not going to take your new sleigh this trip. I'm going to send my reindeer with you and each reindeer will have their very own sleigh wagon to move your Uncle Ken-Buck and his factory to Branson. We'll have Sugar Snow go with you along with Branson the Balladeer, Josh Elf, Harvey, Rene and Elva Elf and whoever else who would want to go to ride in their own sleigh. Then, later when the Pine Cone Chip factory is up and running again, we'll have the reindeer or your family haul Pine Cone Chips from Branson to the North Pole."

"Wow, I'm ready to go now!" says Snowdeer.

Then Santa says, "Let's go get Branson the Balladeer, Josh, Gary, Jennie, Harvey and anyone else who would like to help and be on our way! HO-HO-HO!"

So, off they go to the reindeer barn where they find Josh Elf and Branson the Balladeer singing. Harvey, Jennie and Gary Elf are brushing Santa's reindeer and feeding and watering them.

When they see Santa, Harvey is the first to run up to him and he says, "Ha-Ha-Ha-Ho-Ho-Ho! Santa where do you want us to go?"

Santa says to all of them, "I would like for you all to hitch up the reindeer to their own separate sleigh wagons 'cause we're headed to Branson!"

"Branson?" asks a surprised Branson the Balladeer.

"Yes, my friend, Branson," answers Santa and he continues to tell Branson the Balladeer about Snowdeer's Uncle Ken-Buck moving his factory to Branson.

75

With great excitement Branson the Balladeer says, "I'll get to see my family a lot now. That is with your permission Santa."

Santa smiles and answers, "Yes, Branson, you're welcome to go anytime, but I've got a feeling they're gonna put you to work my friend! HO-HO-HO!"

Branson laughs and says, "Santa, it won't seem like work at all! It'll be fun and so great to see my parents and Dosi Doe and Grandpa Jack and Nana Sherry! How soon can we leave?"

Santa says, "As soon as you get the reindeer and sleigh wagons ready and the elves have picked anyone who wants to go, then you are sure welcome to head out. Let's meet over at the reindeer launch pad and I'll get the Sugar Snow alerted so they can go with you."

"Ha-Ha-Ha-Ho-Ho-Ho! Off to get us ready to go!" says Harvey and then he picks Josh, Branson, Gary and Jennie to go along with Snowdeer, Plum Puddin' and Purple Mouse to guide their own individual sleigh wagons.

They each pick out their own reindeer and harness them to their sleigh wagon. Then they head toward the reindeer launch pad.

Santa, who is already there, says in a loud voice, "SUGAR SNOW! SUGAR SNOW! TODAY, TO BRANSON YOU WILL GO!"

Immediately, the Sugar Snow that had been laying by the North Pole's Pole starts blowing toward Santa. Even the Sugar Snow who had been laying in Santa's magical Sugar Snow trunk in the reindeer barn comes flying out to meet them. The Sugar Snow flies up in the air and then comes down and circles around Santa. Then they stay nearby, floating in the air waiting for their orders.

When Santa sees that every reindeer is hitched to their sleigh wagon and the drivers are holding their reins ready to go, he thinks of something and says, "Harvey, would you go get Taper and Tallow please? I would like them to accompany Snowdeer and you and the gang. That way, when it gets dark, they will light your way."

"Yes sir, Santa," Harvey replies and off he goes in a rush to get the candles.

"Thank you Santa-I really do appreciate it," says Snowdeer.

"You are very welcome Snowdeer. Just looking out for you, My Little Deer!" Santa says and laughs. Snowdeer shakes his head and laughs too.

In the meantime, Harvey has found Taper and Tallow at Snowdeer's Headquarters standing on guard at the entrance door. Harvey says, "Taper! Tallow! Santa wants you to join Snowdeer and the gang to go help Snowdeer's Uncle Ken-Buck move his Pine Cone Chips factory to Branson! Would you join us please?"

"Yes Sir!" Taper and Tallow reply.

Then Harvey says, "Great! Well then, Ha-Ha-Ha-Ho-Ho-Ho! Let's get you ready, with Snowdeer to go!" So off they go to the reindeer take off pad.

After they are safely inside the sleigh that Snowdeer is in, Snowdeer looks at both of them and says, "Thank you for coming, we will sure need your light!"

Both Taper and Tallow say, "Snowdeer, we're happy to serve you."

So, with all the reindeer harnessed to the sleigh wagons and Harvey now back in his sleigh, Santa gets a big grin and with a loud voice he says, "SUGAR SNOW! SUGAR SNOW! TO THE PINE CONE CHIP FACTORY GO!" After Santa gives those orders, the Sugar Snow circles all of the drivers and the riders and off they go! When Strike the Bell sees what is happening, he starts ringing his bell and the North Pole Village townsfolk come out of their houses and look up in the sky to watch the takeoff. They start cheering them on and Santa laughs and says, "Well, there they go! Those North Pole Kingdom flyers are getting this down pretty good! HO-HO-HO! Now, I think I will head to my underground headquarters and see if Miss Tasha has any cookies and milk left and then this ole boy is gonna take me a nap!" So, off he goes to his underground lair for a snack and a nice winters rest.

Meanwhile, Snowdeer and the gang are having another wonderful time flying through the air. But, in a little bit, Harvey shouts, "There's the Seymour Woods below and there's the Pine Cone Chip factory! Let's head down!" So, they all land their sleighs in a clearing in the woods beside the Pine Cone Chip factory. Snowdeer jumps out of his sleigh and rushes to his Uncle Ken-Buck's factory and knocks on the door.

Uncle Ken-Buck opens the door and hugs his nephew and says, "Hello ole boy! It looks like Santa told you the news!"

"Yes Sir, he did," answers Snowdeer. Then he gets a serious look on his face and says to his uncle, "Uncle Ken-Buck, Santa said you had a surprise to tell me. I've got to know. What is it?"

Ken-Buck gets a mischievous look on his face and says, "Snowdeer, why don't you just ask your mother and daddy?" Snowdeer gets a funny look on his face and then his face turns to joy when he sees his daddy Jim-Buck and mother Deerlores step out from a room they had been hiding in.

"Daddy! Momma! What are you doing here?" asks Snowdeer.

Jim-Buck answers, "Well Son, your mother and I have something to tell you. We're going to move and live part time in Branson and part time in Doe Run. We're going to help your Uncle Ken-Buck with his Pine Cone Chips. Since Santa asked him to make more of them to take on your travels, he will need a whole lot of help. Also, this way we'll get to see you more often because we know you'll be coming to Branson to pick them up."

"We sure look forward to helping you and going along on some of your trips!" adds Deerlores.

Snowdeer says, "Wow, that is wonderful! When are you moving?"

"Right now son," answers Jim-Buck.

"Well, I'm ready to help," says Snowdeer.

"Us too!" say all the others.

So, Jim-Buck and Ken-Buck talk among themselves and Jim-Buck says, "Snowdeer, your Momma and I need you to take us to Doe Run to pick up some things and then we'll meet the rest of the gang in Branson."

"Yes Sir!" answers Snowdeer. Then he asks, "Where will you and Momma be staying in Branson?"

Jim-Buck answers, "We will meet with our friends Raine and Hager who live in Branson and they will help us find a place."

Snowdeer says, "Oh Yes! I remember Todd Lott talking about them."

Then Jim-Buck continues, "They have been through Doe Run and Knob Lick lots of times. Raine is a painter and he paints beautiful paintings of people and the Ozarks scenery. His friend Hager travels with him and is a writer of Christian stories and is also an Ozark explorer."

"You think Raine would ever paint me?" asks Snowdeer.

"O, I'm sure he would Snowdeer. And if he does, make sure you load him down with lots of Pine Cone Chips and take him to the North Pole with You so he can paint Santa, Mrs. Santa and the gang!" answers Jim-Buck laughing.

"O, I will do that Daddy," answers Snowdeer.

Then Deerlores says, "Snowdeer, when we get to Doe Run, I'll fix you a big supper and then, we can load up your wagon with all that your father and I need to take to Branson. But, I also want you to pick out some of your favorite things to bring along so that when we have a place in Branson, we'll have a special room for you, and you'll have some of your things there too."

Snowdeer smiles and says, "Thank you Momma. You and Daddy Deer are the best!"

Then Snowdeer turns to everyone and says, "We'll divide up the Sugar Snow and Daddy, Momma, Taper and I will leave now to go pick up things at Doe Run and then meet you all later tonight in Branson. Tallow, Plum Puddin', Purple Mouse, Branson, Harvey and all the rest, please go help Uncle Ken-Buck load up all that he needs and then head to Branson. Take care and see you there!"

Then Snowdeer looks at the Sugar Snow and asks, "Sugar Snow, would part of you please come with me, Momma, Daddy and Taper to Doe Run?"

The Sugar Snow answers with an excited, Yes! And then they fly up in the air and talk among themselves. When they have decided what to do, about a fourth of them come up to Snowdeer and say, "We're here for you Snowdeer and ready to assist!" The other Sugar Snow goes over to Ken-Buck and they tell him they are there for him.

So, everyone says their goodbyes and Snowdeer says, "SUGAR SNOW! SUGAR SNOW! TO THE DOE RUN FOREST WE GO!" And with that, the Sugar Snow circles them and off they go in a rush to Doe Run.

Ken-Buck says to the remaining gang, "Please bring your sleigh wagons up to the factory doors. We have lots of nuts and chocolate to load up! I asked my wife

Jackie-Doe to come and Mark-Buck too. They should have everything in the storeroom lined up and ready for us to take to Branson."

So each one of them loads up their sleigh wagons with so much chocolate, nuts, ingredients and pans that there's almost no room for Ken-Buck to ride!

Ken-Buck looks at the loaded sleigh wagons and laughs and says, "Mommom Evelyn Whitetail always told me to have enough food to go around, and from the looks of our sleigh wagons, we for sure do!"

Everyone laughs and then after everything is loaded and ready to go, Ken-Buck, Plum Puddin', Purple Mouse and Branson the Balladeer look at each other and Plum Puddin' asks, "Who's gonna ask the Sugar Snow to send us off?"

Harvey breaks in and says, "I will!" and then looking around at the Sugar Snow he says, "SUGAR SNOW! SUGAR SNOW! TO THE BRANSON OZARKS GO!" The Sugar Snow rises up and swirls around the reindeer and the riders and the sleigh wagons, and off they go with a Whoosh! Everyone laughs at the speedy departure and the excitement builds. They know within a short time they will see the tiny country community of Branson.

When they arrive, Branson the Balladeer, Plum Puddin' and Purple Mouse hop off their sleighs and run to Reuben Branson's cabin. Wanting to surprise his folks, Branson the Balladeer knocks on the door. As it opens, Reuben and Mary are shocked because they didn't expect them to come back so soon!

Reuben says, "Welcome back! What a pleasant surprise!"

Then Mary says, "Welcome! Let me fix y'all some supper and we'll visit."

Reuben walks over to the sleighs and sees Ken-Buck and Jackie-Doe and he says, "Hello Ken-Buck and Jackie-Doe! I've talked with Raine and Hager already and I think they have a cabin for you all. Let's go pay 'em a visit."

"Ok, we would really appreciate that. Thank you Mr. Branson," answers Ken-Buck.

Then Mary says, "Plum Puddin', would you please go over to Grandpa Jack and Nana Sherry's cabin and invite them for supper? And ask Sherry if she would help me with the cookin'. They'll be surprised to see ya. We can visit while the others are going about their business."

Plum Puddin' says, "Yes, Ma'am, I would be happy to do that!" and off he rushes over to their cabin.

While Reuben, Ken-Buck and Jackie-Doe are on their way to see Raine and Hager, they see in the distance a young couple with a baby walking across a field where the White River and Roark Creek meet.

As they come face to face, Reuben says, "Good evenin' Calvin and Cassandra."

"Good evenin' to you," replies the young father and mother.

Then Reuben says, "Calvin-Cassandra, this is Ken-Buck and his wife Jackie-Doe."

Calvin answers, "Hello, I'm Calvin Gayler and this here's my wife Cassandra and our little one. Nice to meet your acquaintance."

"Pleasure to meet you too," says Ken-Buck and Jackie-Doe.

Then Reuben says, "Calvin and Cassandra are the youngest couple in Branson. He's 15 and she's 14."

"My, you all sure got an early start, and a baby too!" says Jackie-Doe.

"Yes, we sure did start early," answers Cassandra, and then she laughs.

Reuben says, "Ken-Buck and Jackie-Doe are moving here and gonna have a Pine Cone Chip factory." Then he explains how they make the Pine Cone Chips.

Calvin says, "I'm a gunsmith and the Mrs. and me live in a cave just above the White River. I make guns so I can hunt game and keep the bushwhackers away."

"Bushwhackers?" asks Ken-Buck.

"Yes, bushwhackers. That's our Ozark name for criminals," says Calvin.

"Well, in that case, we'll have to be on the lookout for 'em," says Ken-Buck.

"Well, you ain't gonna have to worry too much about that Mr. Buck 'cause Jim Babcock, who's the law here in Taney County, and who's also an Ozark collector of anything having to do with Branson, is always watching for 'em! And Jim, along with his friend, Chick Allen, who is a root and herb man here in the Ozarks, sure know how to shoot a gun!"

They all laugh and Calvin's wife Cassandra says, "Ole Chick. He's a good ole boy. He collects Indian arrowheads and plays music on the jaw-bone of a mule."

"Are you kiddin'?" asks Jackie-Doe.

Calvin replies, "Nope, Miss Jackie, she ain't kiddin'. I've seen him play it a many a time, and after you move here, I'm sure you'll see him play it too."

Then Cassandra says, "When y'all get settled in, we'll have to meet with Jim Babcock and his wife Jean for supper 'cause she's a great cook. And sometime we should meet with her and quilt some bedspreads together."

Jackie-Doe says, "Yes, we would love to meet them and I love to quilt!"

After they talk a little while longer, Calvin looks at the sky and says, "Well, I reckon we'd better get goin'. Got to check the animals before it gets dark."

So they all say their good byes and off to the cave they go.

After Reuben, Ken-Buck and Jackie-Doe start walking again, their path leads them to Lake Taneycomo. Reuben says, "I love this lake. It has miles and miles of shoreline. I love to fish here and go canoeing with my friend Taneycomo."

"Taneycomo?" asks Ken-Buck.

Reuben answers, "Yes, Taneycomo. His parents, Jody and Gordon Wolf are Indian, and they named him Taneycomo after this lake." "We know him. He's our friend," says Ken-Buck.

But before Reuben can say anything else, they all see Raine and Hager coming across the mountain and walking toward them. Reuben waves to them and they wave back, and when they come face to face, Reuben says, "Good evenin' Raine and Hager. This is Ken-Buck and his wife Jackie-Doe. They, along with his brother Jim-Buck and his wife Deerlores, are the ones I was talking to you about that are moving here to Branson."

They greet each other and Hager smiles at them and says, "Yes, we've heard a lot about you and we've been workin' on some cabins for you all to stay in."

Then Raine says, "We really hope you like them. There's a great view of Lake Taneycomo from them."

Reuben says, "The Bucks are also going to need a big cabin to start making their Pine Cone Chips in."

Hager says, "Oh yes, we already talked about that and we're going to build you a new log cabin for that with a big fireplace where you can melt your chocolate and mix it all together."

"Mmmm, you're makin' me hungry for them," says Reuben.

Then Raine says, "That really sounds good to me too! I can't wait to eat some of 'em!"

Ken-Buck says, "I'd like to tell you how all this began and why we are moving here to Branson."

Then he begins to tell Reuben, Raine and Hager how Pine Cone Chips got started and how Snowdeer has an agreement with Santa and them to make Pine Cone Chips to take to the North Pole and then to be delivered around the world. He also tells them how they will take the ingredients to the North Pole and make them up there too!

Raine and Hager get excited with this news and Hager says, "That is wonderful! Do you think we could go to the North Pole sometime?"

Ken-Buck says, "I don't see why not. Santa loves to have visitors and he may even have you do some writing about his Travels Hager!"

Then Ken-Buck looks at Raine and says, "And Santa may put you to work painting murals up there!"

They all laugh and then Reuben says, "Let's go to the other side of the mountain and see the cabins."

So off they go. When they arrive, Ken-Buck and Jackie-Doe's mouths drop open. They see not only two cabins, but a larger log cabin already built, complete with a mural that Raine has painted above the cabin door saying, "The Buck Family's Original Pine Cone Chips."

The Bucks stand there speechless and Raine asks, "Do you like it?"

"Do we like it?" says Ken-Buck. "Yes! It's even better than I dreamed, and we're shocked that it's already built!"

Then Jackie-Doe says, "Now, we can get moved in and start making the Pine Cone Chips! Jim-Buck, Deerlores and Snowdeer will be here tonight and they'll sure be surprised!"

Ken-Buck agrees and says, "Yes, they will dear. Well, let's take a look inside and see what Hager and Raine have built."

So, they go through the three log cabins with smiles on their faces and then they walk back by Lake Taneycomo to Reuben and Mary's cabin for supper, thrilled that they now have a home and a factory in Branson.

25 - SNOWDEER'S COMIN'

Meanwhile, Snowdeer and his daddy Jim-Buck and momma Deerlores and the family are having supper at their cabin in the Doe Run forest. They've already loaded up the sleigh and the Sugar Snow is eagerly waiting for their cue to start flying south to Branson.

Jim-Buck says, "You know, I'm gonna miss not being in the Doe Run Forest as much, but the way I see it, life will be even better, seeing Snowdeer more and working with the family in the Pine Cone Chip business."

"Yes, I agree," says Deerlores. "I love the Ozark Mountains of Doe Run and Branson. And now it will be a great experience, getting to live at both places."

Snowdeer says, "I can hardly wait to get there! Can we go now?"

Jim-Buck and Deerlores both say yes, so they all hurry and finish their supper, go outside to harness up the reindeer and load up sleighs.

Then Snowdeer says, "Let's say the magic words and head to Branson!"

So, after he tells them the magic words to say, he counts them off...1....2....3....and they all say, "HO-HO-HO! OFF TO BRANSON WE GO!"

The Sugar Snow immediately flies upward, then comes down and circles and swirls around them and off the ground they rise and take off in a big Whoosh! They all laugh as they fly upward and over to Branson.

Jim-Buck hollers to Deerlores, "I think the Sugar Snow's more excited to get there than we are!"

And after what seemed like only minutes, they look down and see Lake Taneycomo and Reuben Branson's cabin.

"There it is!" shouts Snowdeer.

In the meantime down below, Plum Puddin' and Purple Mouse have eaten and are swinging in Reuben Branson's swing. All of a sudden, they both hear something and they look up and see Snowdeer and the gang flying in. Plum Puddin' and Purple Mouse holler to them and then jump off the swing and run to the cabin door and holler, "Snowdeer's comin'!"

Everyone rushes out to see them, and as they gather on the porch of the log cabin, Snowdeer's sleigh lands safely on the grass in front of them. Snowdeer, Deerlores, Jim-Buck and the family jump out of their sleighs and greet the gang who have been waiting for them.

Reuben says, "Welcome Jim-Buck, Deerlores, Snowdeer and family! Would you like to see your new cabin?"

"Yes Sir!," answers Jim-Buck.

Then Reuben says, "Ok, let's head over to the mountain and take a look!"

So, they all take off for the mountain by Lake Taneycomo and as they come over the top, they see the new Pine Cone Chip factory cabin as well as the other two cabins! Their eyes open wide and their mouths open even wider!

"Whoa!" says Snowdeer and Deerlores' eyes fill with tears.

Jim-Buck just stands there shaking his head! Raine and Hager walk up to him and ask how he likes it. Jim-Buck replies, "It's more than I ever thought it would be and we didn't realize it would be finished already! Thank you very much!"

Ken-Buck comes up and gives Jim-Buck a slap on the back and says, "Brother, we're gonna make more Pine Cone Chips here than we have ever made in our lives, and they're gonna go all around the world! And, Jackie-Doe and I want to make you and Deerlores our partners!"

"What? your partners?" asks Jim-Buck.

"Yes Sir, Mr. Buck," answers Ken-Buck. Ken-Buck looks at Deerlores and then back at Jim-Buck and says, "So, what's your answer?"

Jim-Buck looks at Deerlores and smiles. She nods and smiles back and they both answer at the same time, "We're in!"

Everyone starts clapping and yelling Yay!

So, they all go through the cabins and then the Pine Cone Chip factory cabin. Jim-Buck, Deerlores, Snowdeer and the family love it all and can't wait to get settled in and start making the Pine Cone Chips!

After they have come back outside, Grandpa Jack walks up to Ken-Buck and Jim-Buck and puts a hand on each of their shoulders and says, "You boys are gonna make a lot of silver doin' this!" They all laugh and then head back to Reuben and Mary's cabin to celebrate this special occasion.

26 - EXCITEMENT AT GRANDPA JACK
AND NANA SHERRY'S CABIN

Later that night after visiting some more and having some of Mary and
Sherry's country cookin', they decide to call it a night and go to bed. Reuben,
Mary, Jack and Sherry see the large group and decide to divide them up to
stay at their cabins. They make pallets for each of them and the floors are
covered wall to wall with friends. After telling them where the outhouse is, they all
go to sleep.

The next morning, at both cabins, they wake up to the smell of ham and
eggs and homemade biscuits.

Plum Puddin' says, "Mmmmm" and jumps out of his pallet.

They all follow his lead and meet at the table by the fireplace to eat.

Then Plum Puddin' says, "Thank You Mr. and Mrs. Branson. We sure do
appreciate you letting us stay."

Reuben and Mary both say that he is welcome and that they are invited to
come back and stay with them anytime they want.

Over at Grandpa Jack and Nana Sherry's cabin, Grandpa Jack had just said
grace and breakfast was being served, when they begin to hear a noise outside. Their
dog Lickerish had dug a ditch under the fence and had gotten into the pigpen to eat
some of the pigs' food. The pigs had gotten excited, started running, broke down the
gate and got into the chicken yard. Pigs were gruntin', the chickens were squawkin'
and feathers were flyin'!

Everybody at the Branson's cabin can hear the commotion. Plum Puddin'
and his dog Pinecone run down to see what's going on. Grandpa Jack and Nana
Sherry come running out of their cabin, and when they see what's happening, they
begin to separate the pigs from the chickens trying to get the pigs back in their pen.
Plum Puddin' joins in and soon they get all the animals back in the right places.
Then they get the fence and the gate fixed. Lickerish, after seeing what he had
started, had taken off running and was hiding under the porch.

Grandpa Jack laughs and says, "Well, that's enough excitement for one day!
Everyone, come back in the cabin and we'll finish our breakfast!"

When they are done, Grandpa Jack says, "Let's go over to Reuben's cabin
and see what they've got planned for today."

After their guests have thanked Nana Sherry for the meal, they all walk over
to the Branson's cabin and Grandpa Jack knocks on the door.

Reuben opens the door and says, "Come on in everyone! We're just finishin' up breakfast! Plum Puddin' came back and said y'all had some excitement in the barnyard".

Grandpa Jack answers, "Yes, we did, but we have it all fixed now."

"Good!" says Reuben.

Then Grandpa Jack asks, "What do you have goin' on for today Reuben?"

Reuben replies, "Well, today is a special day 'cause Snowdeer, Plum Puddin' and the gang are headed back to the North Pole."

Then Grandpa Jack says, "Let us know what we can do to help."

Reuben answers, "Ok, thank you," and then turns to Snowdeer and says, "Snowdeer, let's go now and get your parents and Ken-Buck and Jackie's things unloaded from the sleigh wagons. They'll be stayin' for a while so we'll get them settled in their cabins and then unload all the ingredients for the Pine Cone Chips at the Pine Cone Chip factory."

"Yes sir," says Snowdeer.

So everyone helps get them unloaded and then they meet back at Reuben's cabin so they can leave for the North Pole. After everyone has said their goodbyes, they get in their sleigh wagons and Snowdeer asks the Sugar Snow, "Are you ready?"

The Sugar Snow starts flying up in the air and makes themselves ready for Snowdeer's orders to take all the gang back to the North Pole.

Then Snowdeer says to his Momma Deerlores and his Daddy Jim-Buck, "I love you both and I will be back to see you soon." He looks at Plum Puddin', Purple Mouse and the others and says, "Does everyone know the magic words that will cause us to fly?" Everyone answers, "Yes!" and then Snowdeer says, "Ok, altogether now! "SUGAR SNOW, SUGAR SNOW! OFF TO THE NORTH POLE WE GO!" and the Sugar Snow starts swirling around the sleigh wagons and then they fly up to the deer who are flying the sleighs and swirl around them! Then, with a big "WHOOSH!" they lift up off the ground and take off to the north! Jim-Buck, Deerlores, Ken-Buck, Jackie-Doe, the Branson's and Grandpa Jack and Nana Sherry all wave goodbye and watch as Snowdeer and the gang quickly soar out of sight.

27 - ANOTHER SUGAR SNOW LIGHT SHOW
EUGENIO'S ITALIAN ICE

As they race toward the North Pole, Purple Mouse hollers over to Snowdeer, "Do you think the Sugar Snow would mind putting us on another light show?"

Snowdeer answers, "I don't think they would mind at all. They love doing light shows and I'd love to see them do another one myself! Let's see if they will." So, Snowdeer looks around at the Sugar Snow and asks, "Sugar Snow, would you care doing a light show for us this morning please? I know it isn't dark out, but the sun is hid behind the clouds and it isn't real bright, so would you consider maybe doing . . ."

Before Snowdeer could finish his sentence, the Sugar Snow starts laughing and swirling around him and the gang and then goes up in the air and start turning different colors! They still shine with amazing light, even though it's during the day! Russ Elf turns on the Magical Music Box and they immediately feel like it's Christmas time again! Everyone smiles and giggles in glee and Pinecone starts barking as they're serenaded back to Santa land!

The Sugar Snow circles the gang and then goes high up in the sky, making formations of Christmas things like candy canes, gingerbread men, pieces of candy and taffy, and shapes like Pine Cone Chips! This brings so much joy to the gang that they totally forget about the time and they don't realize they're almost back to Santa's!

Then, the Sugar Snow spells the name, "NORTH POLE" and makes the shape of an arrow moving forward. It is then that the gang realizes they are almost home!

In a little bit, they enter the North Pole Village and hear Strike the Bell ringing and welcoming them home! They see the landing pad below with people all around watching them arrive! After a smooth landing, they look over and see Santa and Mrs. Claus rushing over to greet them.

Santa says, "HO-HO-HO! Welcome Home! We've missed you!"

Then Snowdeer says, "It's great to see you Santa, Mrs. Claus and everyone else! We've missed you too!"

Then Mrs. Claus says, "Santa and I have talked and we've agreed that this calls for a celebration! Tonight, we're gonna have Josh, Melody and Dale Elf play a big North Pole Dance at Elf Hall and we'll have all kinds of goodies and special snow cones for desert from Eugenio's Italian Ice. Mr. Eugenio is a snowman and his beautiful snowwoman wife have run their business for years with their snow family right here at the North Pole."

Santa taps Mrs. Claus on the shoulder and with a big grin he says, "My dear, did you know their slogan is, "There's SNOW order so big that God and us can't handle?"

Everyone laughs and Snowdeer says, "That sounds great to me Santa! Makes me want a snow cone right now!" Everyone laughs again and Snowdeer says to Santa, "I'm sure looking forward to tonight's program. Do you think they'll play Christmas Party Square Dance Song?"

Santa answers, "I'm sure they would be happy to do it for you, but I'll request it, just to make sure they do." Then Santa looks at everyone and says, "See You all tonight at Elf Hall at 7 Pm–with jingle bells on! HO-HO-HO!"

28 - SPEAKING IN RIDDLES
SANTA'S COMPASS ROOM

As the North Pole villagers go about their business, Santa looks at the gang and says, "Let's head over to my underground Headquarters. I have some more things I want to tell you about before the Dance tonight."

So, the gang starts walking over to his underground lair. On the way, Taper and Tallow begin to light with the excitement of being home and knowing that going to Santa's lair means there will be another trip soon! As they walk down the big long staircase, Taper and Tallow's candle lights cast shadows on the secret passageway.

All of a sudden, Santa sees something moving out of the corner of his eye. He instantly knows who it is and grinning he says, "Ok Riddle, you can come out now. I saw you my friend!" So, out from the corner comes an elf with white hair and neatly dressed in a brown suit trimmed in red, green and silver. Santa says, "Hello Riddle, How are you today?"

Riddle answers, "I'm doing great Santa! Life's just one big joke!" and then he laughs. Everyone laughs with him and Santa introduces Riddle to everyone and tells them that Riddle lives up to his name. Riddle gets a mischievous look on his face and says, "Yes, my name is Riddle and I'm into Riddles and Puns. Wanna hear one?" Santa, Snowdeer and all nod yes and then he asks, "You all know what you get when you're locked up in a closet with Santa?"

"No, what?" asks Snowdeer.

"CLAUSTROPHOBIA!" answers Riddle laughing.

Santa rolls his eyes and says, "I've heard that one a million times, but I still like it! HO-HO-HO!"

Riddle continues, "Here's another one. Mrs. Claus asks Santa how the weathers gonna be that day. Santa replies, "It looks like it's gonna, "REINDEER!"

"HO-HO-HO!" Santa belly laughs and all the rest crack up too. Taper and Tallow laugh so hard they blow their candles out!

Riddle looks at them and says, "Hey, don't leave us in the dark!" After he says that, Snowdeer laughs and snorts and immediately Riddle says, "Did I hear a little, "BUCK SNORT?"

They all crack up again and Santa says, "Plum Puddin' when you, Snowdeer and Purple Mouse go back to Branson, PLEASE take him with you! HO-HO-HO!"

"No way!" the three of them answer back and then laugh.

Purple Mouse has laughed so hard that he starts turning purple. Not knowing Purple Mouse could do that, Riddle jumps back and gives him a funny look and Plum Puddin' says, "Riddle, if you think that's something, just wait till he sees Tasha Mouse!"

Riddle laughs and tries to think of a comeback joke, but stops when he sees Purple Mouse turning an even deeper purple while staring down the stairs. "What are you blushing about?" asks Riddle and then they all see Tasha Mouse at the end of the staircase holding a lantern. "Oh, I see what you mean," says Riddle and they all laugh.

Purple Mouse just looks down and says, "Oops."

Then, they walk down the rest of the stairs and meet up with Tasha and Santa says, "Tasha my dear, would you bring us the World Traveler Logbook please?"

"Yes Sir, Santa," answers Tasha and off she goes.

Santa says, "I have another part of my secret lair I have never shown you. It's my Magical Compass Room." Plum Puddin', Snowdeer and Purple Mouse look at each other and grin and Santa says, "Let's go there and Tasha will meet us."

As they get to a large red and green door with the markings of a compass on it with all points of north, south, east and west, they notice the directions pointer starting to spin. It goes around and around and then stops and points straight north. They watch as the big door starts squeaking and slowly opening.

Santa gets a smile and says, "Let's go on in!"

By then, Tasha Mouse had gathered the World Traveler Log Book and joins them. Once inside, they marvel at such a big tall room filled with world maps and books about all of the countries, cities, and country communities.

"Wow, Santa, why haven't you shown us this room before?" asks Snowdeer.

"Well, Snowdeer, Santa doesn't show everything all at once. There's only so much you can take in at one time and I wanted to wait and show this special room to you now. The longer you know me, the more surprises you will see! HO-HO-HO!"

"I'm beginning to see what you mean Santa," says Snowdeer.

"I know that always keeps me coming back," jokes Plum Puddin'.

"Well, my dear boy, as long as you keep bringing that Plum Pudding, I'll keep bringing the surprises," says Santa laughing. Then he turns to look at Snowdeer and asks, "Are you ready for your first real trip as my ambassador Snowdeer?"

"Yes Sir, Santa," replies Snowdeer.

Then Santa says, "Ok, then HO-HO-HO! Here we go! But, before you find out where you will be going, I want you all to know another secret."

Then he goes over to a huge telescope and says, "My elves, Rene & Elva use this big magical telescope all during the year and they look over all the world looking to see who needs help the most. When they find those who need lots of help, they tell Tasha, who writes it down in the World Traveler Log and then they pass it on to me. I look at it and then secretly go visit during the year and leave something for them. I can't get around to everyone all the time because the needs are too great. So, this is now an important part your job will be Snowdeer, Plum Puddin' and Purple Mouse."

Snowdeer says, "I understand why it would be too much because of all the new ones being born all the time Santa."

Then Plum Puddin' says, "We will be honored to help as much as we can."

Purple Mouse says, "Santa, thank You for allowing us to help you. We will do our best."

Santa smiles and says, "Thank you for your help. It is sure appreciated!" Then Santa looks at Snowdeer and says, "Snowdeer, Taper and Tallow will need to go with you on your trips so they can light your way to help you see at night. You can also have Rene Elf, Elva Elf, Harvey Elf or whoever else you choose to go with you to help you out on your travels. Russ Elf can go and keep you in music, Bev Elf will keep you covered in prayer and whenever Riddle is with you, he'll keep you in jokes!"

They all laugh and then Santa gets a big grin and after pointing to the World Map, he says, "The big World Map above us will light up showing us where in the world you need to go."

"Wow, that's wonderful," says Snowdeer.

"Do you ever have more than one country light up at once?" asks Purple Mouse.

"Yes, we do," answers Santa. Then he speaks to the large world map on the wall and says, "World Map! Show us where Snowdeer needs to go!"

Immediately, a big compass needle in the center of the World Map starts spinning and all of the countries begin to light up. As the needle spins and points to each country, it lights up and then goes dark when the needle moves on to the next country. As the countries blink on and off with the movement of the compass needle, first one country, and then another, everyone wonders which country will remain lit when the light show ends. Then, all of a sudden, the spinning compass stops and Snowdeer's first real flight location is revealed.

"England!" Snowdeer shouts. The whole gang cheers and Taper and Tallow's wicks light up with excitement. Snowdeer asks, "When do we go Santa?"

"Tomorrow," Santa answers. "After we have our party tonight, let's get a good night's sleep and meet at Noon tomorrow at your Headquarters Snowdeer."

"Yes Sir," answers Snowdeer.

Then Santa says, "Snowdeer, I want to tell you that your own world map in your Headquarters will also light up with this one so you will always know where you are to go."

"Thank you very much Santa," says Snowdeer.

"You're very welcome," answers Santa. Then he continues, "That's all for today. I'm going to get Mrs. Claus and the musicians and get tonight's party lined up. See you tonight at 7 Pm over at Elf Hall."

They all say, "Yes Sir, Santa," and then Santa leaves.

Snowdeer looks at Plum Puddin' and Purple Mouse and says, "Can you believe it? We're going to fly to England!"

Then Plum Puddin' pets Pinecone and says, "Isn't that great boy?" Pinecone looks at Plum Puddin' and answers back barking and then lays on his back so Plum Puddin' can rub his belly.

Then Snowdeer says, "Hey! Race you to our Headquarters! 1-2-3-GO!" And off they run followed slowly by Taper and Tallow who won't run because they don't want their candles to blow out.

29 - CHRISTMAS PARTY
SQUARE DANCE SONG

Promptly at 7 Pm, Snowdeer, Plum Puddin', Purple Mouse, Carrot and the gang meet Santa at Elf Hall for the Dance. Josh, Melody and Dale Elf begin singing and playing their hearts out to a full house of cheering North Pole folks. Santa had the De'Neui Family serve a big buffet and Krull's Confectionary, Marquart's Molasses, Dunn's Christmas Buns and Eugenio's Italian Ice went all out serving the best deserts. Plummer's Reindeer Hardware had brought chairs and tables and every seat was filled.

While watching everyone eat to their hearts content, Henry at Body by Dorn says to Plum Puddin', "Tomorrow, business is going to be great 'cause they'll be coming to my place to work it off!"

While they both share a laugh, in walks Melinda Mew, along with her father Bartholomew and his wife Deborah Lew Mew and son Hugh Mew and the rest of the Mew Family Singers. All 100 plus of them! After seeing them come in, Snowdeer asks them to sing, "The Good Mews of Christmas."

"Why yes, we'd be happy to," answers Deborah Lew and Bartholomew, and so the whole cat family goes up to the stage and starts singing it. A big hush comes over the crowd, and the Sugar Snow flies over from the North Pole's Pole and circles around them and the crowd and then goes up in the air and puts on a beautiful light show while the Mew Family sings. The audience is mesmerized, and when the song is over, the crowd goes wild.

Then, Snowdeer hollers out, "Do Christmas Party Square Dance Song!" The crowd wants to hear it too, and they join Snowdeer shouting, "Christmas Party Square Dance Song! Christmas Party Square Dance Song over and over! Josh, Melody and Dale Elf go right into the song and everyone divides up into square dance partners and they start to clap and sing and swing their partners!

"What a joyful time everyone is having tonight! I don't want it to end," says Bev Elf to Russ Elf. Russ Elf completely agrees and then swirls her around.

When the evening does start coming to an end, Santa walks to center stage and says, "Thank you everyone for coming tonight! But, before we leave, Snowdeer, Plum Puddin', Purple Mouse, Carrot and Harvey, please come forward." So, the five friends walk to the center stage and Santa continues, "Snowdeer and his friends will be taking off tomorrow for their first real trip as ambassadors of peace and goodwill to the world!" The crowd cheers again and Santa continues, "I've asked them to go and meet with folks, be they Royals or peasant, rich or poor, young or old to be a

Christmas beacon of God's love to as many as they can talk with. Snowdeer will drive his sleigh and if he ever wants to pull his sleigh, I give my complete blessing for Plum Puddin', Purple Mouse, Harvey or Carrot to drive it."

The four of them look at each other and get the widest grins and then they start thanking Santa as the North Pole Villagers cheer again.

Then Santa continues, "The Krull, Marquart, Dorn and Plummer Family Elves have agreed to be the official Snowdeer support team by helping to wrap presents, shine the sleigh, and to load it when necessary. Harvey, Branson the Balladeer, Josh Elf and Avery Elf will make sure the reindeer are ready to go and if any of Snowdeer's family come up from Doe Run or Branson, they will also help make sure they're ready too. So, let's give them a round of applause."

The crowd hollers and claps and then Santa asks, "Would everyone like to know where they will be flying tomorrow?"

The crowd answers, "Yes!"

Santa tells them, "England!" Once again, the crowd goes wild with cheers and then Santa says, "The gang will meet tomorrow at Noon to get ready for take-off, and all of you are invited. God bless and see you tomorrow. Good night, my dear North Polers! HO-HO-HO!"

Everyone smiles and answers Santa saying, "Good night!" and then they start leaving Elf Hall with excitement in their hearts as they look forward to the special event coming the next day.

Snowdeer, Plum Puddin', Purple Mouse and Carrot thank Santa again, tell him good night and then start walking back to Snowdeer's Headquarters at Bayberry Bay. As they reach the Headquarters, they stop to take in the beautiful sights and they begin to wonder. With the sweet scents of the bay filling the air, and the excitement of the upcoming day, will they ever be able to go to sleep?

30 - TERRIE YOUNG DEER AND TANEYCOMO'S SECRET SURPRISE

Early the next morning, Snowdeer wakes up to the sound of Taper and Tallow knocking on his bedroom door.

"Time to wake up, world traveler! Breakfast is ready," they say.

So, Snowdeer opens one eye and takes a peek at the Snowdeer clock Santa made him to see what time it is. He suddenly remembers today they are going to England, so he quickly jumps out of bed and takes off running to the door and out to the dining room where he finds Plum Puddin' eating Plum Pudding, Carrot the rabbit eating carrots and lettuce, and Purple Mouse feasting on a variety of cheeses.

Plum Puddin' looks at Snowdeer and says, "We got this food as a surprise gift today and here's your surprise!"

Plum Puddin' raises the table cloth and out pops Terrie Young Deer holding a great big horn of plenty filled with nuts, berries and other things Snowdeer loves!

A shocked Snowdeer says, "Terrie Young Deer! How did you get here?"

Terrie Young Deer smiles and replies, "Santa and Mrs. Santa were out flying early this morning taking a little trip to the Ozarks. Taneycomo and I were canoeing on Lake Taneycomo, when all of a sudden we heard something above us, and when we looked up, we saw them flying toward us. After they landed, they walked over to Reuben and Mary Branson's cabin and visited with them for a while and then they went over to Grandpa Jack and Nana Sherry's cabin and had a nice long visit with them. Then, they came over where we were floating and after visiting a while, Santa asked if I would like to come up to see you and the gang, and I said yes! I asked the Clauses if I could bring these gifts to you, along with another special gift."

"Another gift?" asks Snowdeer.

"Yes, and there it is," says Terrie Young Deer as she points to a trunk in the corner. Right after she says that, up pops the lid of the big trunk and Taneycomo jumps up and gives a war whoop, surprising them all.

An excited Snowdeer says, "Welcome Taneycomo! Great to see you!"

Taneycomo replies, "Great to see you too Snowdeer. We come long way. Santa faster than canoe!" Then they all have a good laugh.

Snowdeer says, "Yes, Santa is definitely faster than a canoe! No one can outrun Santa and his reindeer once he throws Sugar Snow on 'em!" They all laugh again and Snowdeer asks Taneycomo and Terrie Young Deer, "Did Santa tell you the news about us going to England?"

"Yes, he did," they both answer. Then Terrie Young Deer says, "We are so happy for you and what you and the gang are doing here at the North Pole."

Taneycomo says, "We plan on watching you take off today before going back to float again in Lake Taneycomo. It takes something pretty special like this to get me out of a canoe," Taneycomo jokes.

They all laugh and Snowdeer says, "Thank you all very much for bringing all the goodies. We really appreciate it. Whatever is left over from breakfast I'll leave in the horn of plenty and take it on the sleigh so we can eat it on the way!"

Then Snowdeer gets an idea and he says to Terrie Young Deer and Taneycomo, "Stay with us, and after breakfast we'll take you on a tour around the North Pole and we'll visit with some of our friends before we go over to the Reindeer Barn to get ready to take off for England."

"We would love that Snowdeer," says Terrie Young Deer and Taneycomo agrees.

So, after everyone had eaten, they go walking around the North Pole Village visiting with Snowdeer's friends and then they venture over to the Reindeer Barn.

31 - MORE DEER SURPRISES

As they arrive at the front of the Reindeer Barn, they find Santa and Mrs. Claus with the Krull, Marquart, Dorn and Plummer Family elves, who are shining up Snowdeer's sleigh while it's sitting on the take-off pad.

Santa sees Snowdeer and the gang coming, and he asks, "How does it look?"

Everyone smiles real big and Snowdeer answers, "It looks perfect Santa. We're really looking forward to this trip." Then he looks at the elves who have been working hard on his sleigh, and he says to them, "Thank you all for your hard work, the sleigh looks wonderful!" But then Snowdeer notices there are no reindeer harnessed to the sleigh and he asks Santa, "Who's gonna pull the sleigh Sir? Where are your reindeer?"

Santa laughs and says, "HO-HO-HO! I knew I forgot something," and then winks at Mrs. Claus.

Then Mrs. Claus looks at Snowdeer and says, "Snowdeer, we thought with this being your first official trip, you would want some special folks to help you out, so we brought in some special help for you."

After she says this, out the door Harvey the Elf runs, along with Josh, Amber, Lilly Kay and Ilsa Marie Elf, Branson The Balladeer, Dosi Doe, Todd Lott, Snowdeer's parents Jim-Buck and Deerlores, his sister Rosie, his brothers Deerell, Antler and Longnose and his Uncle Ken-Buck and Aunt Jackie-Doe! Snowdeer's mouth drops open as he sees his family and friends, and he starts counting them, 1-2-3 ....

Then he puts a hoof to his head and says, "Wow! We're gonna have a full team!" and then he gets to wondering about them being there, and he asks, "How did you all get away? I thought you all were setting up the Pine Cone Chip factory in Branson."

Jim-Buck answers, "Yes, we were son, but when Santa came down to Branson and offered Reuben, Grandpa Jack and us a trip up here to see you....."

"Reuben? Grandpa Jack?" Snowdeer asks. But, before Jim-Buck can answer, Reuben and Mary Branson and Grandpa Jack and Nana Sherry walk out the Reindeer Barn door. Snowdeer laughs and then looks at Santa and says, "O my, you keep the surprises comin', don't you Santa?"

Santa grins at Snowdeer, laughs and answers, "HO-HO-HO! O yes! ... My little deer!" and then laughs again.

Snowdeer laughs too and shakes his head. Then, Tasha Mouse comes through the Reindeer Barn door and says, "Hello everyone, have I missed anything?" When her eyes meet Purple Mouse's eyes, he begins to blush in his purple color once again.

Snowdeer sees it, and he looks at Purple Mouse and kids him saying, "You're blushing! ... My little mouse!" and this makes Purple Mouse blush even more.

Everyone laughs and Santa says, "HO-HO-HO! Now that everyone is here, let's get this sleigh going and spread some good cheer around the world!"

"Yea!" they all shout, and then they hear a multitude of cheers join in behind them. Santa, Snowdeer and the gang hadn't noticed, but while they had been talking, the whole town had turned out to see Snowdeer's first official flight.

32 – BUCKINGHAM, ENGLAND

Santa and Josh hitch Jim-Buck, Deerlores, Ken-Buck, Jackie-Doe, Deerell, Rosie, Antler, Longnose, Dosi Doe and Branson The Balladeer to Snowdeer's sleigh and then Snowdeer jumps in and grabs the reins.

Santa says, "Bev Elf, would you please say a special prayer for safety and then Russ Elf, would you please jump in the sleigh and turn on the Magical Music Box right after the prayer?"

"We'd be happy to, Santa," they answer.

Then Santa says, "Taper and Tallow, would you please climb into the sleigh and take your places on each side of Snowdeer. That way, you'll each be in the perfect positions to give him light so he can see at night."

"Yes Sir Santa," they both reply.

Then Santa says, "Plum Puddin', Purple Mouse, Carrot, and Pinecone, would you please climb into the sleigh and after a few more things, we'll be on our way! HO-HO-HO!" Santa looks over and sees Tasha who is holding a compass and asks her to bring it to him. He takes it and then turning toward the gang he says, "This is a Magical Compass and it will help you stay in the right direction." Then he looks at Rene and Elva Elf and asks, "Would you hand me the Map please?"

"Yes Sir," they both say and then they hand Santa the Map.

"Thank you ladies," Santa says to them as he takes the Map and then tells everyone, "Rene and Elva Elf have what I call, the Magical Map. They will be taking it along to show you which stops to make in England, or on any other journey you may be sent on. So, we have a Magical Compass to lead you all in the right direction and the Magical Map that will show where you are to go." The people cheer and Santa hands the Compass and Map to Carrot, Plum Puddin' and Purple Mouse and then says, "I want you to always be watching the Compass and the Map so you will be prepared to tell Snowdeer what direction he is to go and where his stops will be. Will you do that please?"

"Yes Sir," they all answer.

Then Santa says to Rene and Elva Elf, "Ladies, please climb into the sleigh. We are ready to go my dears." After they have entered the sleigh, Santa looks around and says to the Sugar Snow, "Sugar Snow, are you ready to go to England?"

The Sugar Snow lights up and swirls around Santa and in little voices they say, "Yes Sir!"

Then Santa says, "HO-HO-HO! Everybody say this together. "SUGAR SNOW! SUGAR SNOW! OFF TO THE COUNTRY OF ENGLAND GO!"

After saying that, the Sugar Snow swirls around Snowdeer and the rest of the gang and around the sleigh and then up they rise off the landing pad. Then, with a big WHOOSH! they take off for England.

As they fly over the North Pole, they feel the cold Arctic air blowing past them. Then they start flying into the clouds. What a thrill it is for all of them to fly through the fluffy overcast sky! As they fly upward and come out on the upper side of the clouds, they see the beautiful sun shining above them. Russ Elf keeps the music playing on the Magical Music Box and the Sugar Snow keeps flying alongside the team of deer and the sleigh. They all smile and laugh as they soar through the sky!

In a little bit, Carrot, who is holding the Magical Map says, "According to Santa's Map, we are above the Arctic Ocean. Then, after a little while, Carrot sees something coming into view. Not knowing what it is, he checks the Map, then he says, "Look to the right everyone! Greenland is coming into view!"

They all admire the view and Elva Elf says, "Wow! Greenland is almost completely covered with ice!" Plum Puddin', who is holding the Magical Compass, notices it starting to spin and then stops as it begins to point east.

He then announces to the group, "The Compass shows we are to head east."

Rene Elf, who is watching the Magical Map with Carrot says, "The Map now shows we will be flying by Norway soon."

When they approach Norway, Snowdeer asks the team of deer to fly lower so they can see it up close. As the deer start heading downward everyone sees snowcapped mountains and castles. "What a beautiful sight," says Snowdeer. A while later, Plum Puddin' watches as the Magical Compass starts spinning around and around and then it stops and shows they are to head southeast.

Carrot announces, "The Map shows that we are flying over the North Atlantic Ocean. At this rate, we should be in England by sundown."

"That's great!" says Taper. "That means soon Tallow and I will be able to use our candlelight!"

Some hours later, Plum Puddin's Magical Compass starts spinning again, and once again it points southeast. Purple Mouse grins and says, "I guess the Magical Compass wants us to make sure we keep going in the right direction. I guess that's because it knows Snowdeer's driving!" Then Purple Mouse laughs and elbows Snowdeer in fun. Snowdeer just keeps looking ahead and without missing a beat, he puts a hoof on Purple Mouse's shoulder and acts like he's going to push him overboard.

Then Snowdeer says, "Purple Mouse, Do you know how to swim?" Everyone laughs and Purple Mouse says, "No ... My little deer!" and they all laugh again.

Carrot, who is holding the Magical Map, all of a sudden sees it lighting up. It startles him and he almost drops it out of the sleigh! But, after checking it out, he excitedly tells the gang, "The Map shows we will be coming to Scotland and Ireland and we'll be flying over the Irish Sea." Right after Carrot says that, they look ahead and see land approaching. Then Carrot says, "Look to the left! That's the highlands of Scotland!"

Then, in a little bit, Plum Puddin' says, "Look to the right! There's Ireland!" Then he turns to Snowdeer and asks, "Can we fly lower so we can see it better Snowdeer?"

"Yes, I would be happy to Plum," answers Snowdeer. So, as Snowdeer gives the command to go lower, Russ Elf cranks the Magical Music Box and it begins playing Celtic music. The whole gang loves the music and admires the beautiful green country with its warmer temperatures and beautiful mountains.

"I never dreamed I would ever get to fly around the world, and especially with my special friends!" says Purple Mouse.

"I didn't either," answers Carrot.

Then Plum Puddin', while looking at the Map says, "Hey, according to the Map, we're comin' up to the Irish Sea and then England is next."

"We're almost there," Jim-Buck says to Deerlores as they fly side by side.

Deerlores answers, "Yes dear, we are and what memories we're making! Our first trip around the world and hopefully this is one of many that we'll be making with Snowdeer."

Plum Puddin's Magical Compass starts going around and around again, and once again when it stops, it shows them to continue going southeast. Plum delivers the message to Snowdeer, who in turn relays it on to the other deer. The Sugar Snow starts circling around all of them and giving them an extra boost of energy that makes them immediately start to speed up. After a little while, the Compass goes around and around again, but this time it goes out of control, and to Plum Puddin's surprise, the Compass opens up and the spring comes popping out the back of it!

"OH NO!" says Plum Puddin', "What do we do now?"

Snowdeer quickly replies, "When we get to England, we'll hunt for someone to put it back together." Just after Snowdeer says this, he looks ahead and sees land. "England!" he shouts. All the gang cheer as they cross the Irish Sea shoreline to the country of England.

After they have flown inland for a while, Snowdeer says, "Let's land somewhere and find someone to fix the compass.

So they start looking for the perfect place to land. Purple Mouse spots a great place and he starts pointing to a clearing in the middle of the woods that opens up into a beautiful English countryside.

Snowdeer sees it and says, "Thank You Purple Mouse, that's the perfect place. That's where we'll land."

Then Plum Puddin' reminds Snowdeer, "Remember, the Sugar Snow can cover us and make us invisible so no one will see us, if we ever need to do that."

"Oh yea, thank you for the reminder Plum and yes, we will do that if we have to," answers Snowdeer.

The Sugar Snow overhears what was said and one of them flies up to Snowdeer and Plum Puddin' and says, "We heard you and yes, we will cover you anytime you want. Just say the word."

After they land, the gang jumps out of Snowdeer's sleigh and Plum Puddin', Purple Mouse and Carrot unhitch the deer. They have some of the Sugar Snow stay behind and hide the sleigh, making it invisible to everyone but them. Then they start walking toward the village.

As they get there, Purple Mouse looks at the Magical Map that is lighting up and then he looks at the village sign and says, "Who would have guessed? According to the Map, we were supposed to stop here where we would meet a ...

"Hello mates. How are you today?"

They look to the side of the country lane and just inside the wooded area stands a big English Red Stag deer.

The deer continues, "Welcome to Nottingham. My name is Buckingham. Where are you folks from?"

Startled at seeing another deer in another country who is so friendly, Snowdeer replies, "Hello Mr. Buckingham, my name is Snowdeer and we're here from the North Pole."

Buckingham gets a look of disbelief on his face and he starts to walk away, but Snowdeer runs up behind him and says, "Please, I am telling you the truth sir. We really are from the North Pole and we need your help."

Buckingham turns around and sees that Snowdeer is genuine and he asks, "Why are you here? It isn't Christmas and Santa Claus didn't come with you."

Snowdeer and Plum Puddin' explain the whole story to Buckingham. They explain how they met. They tell Buckingham about the North Pole and Santa and how they have come by special request from Santa to see who needs help and to spread peace and good cheer to their country.

Buckingham gets so excited at hearing their story and he says, "You must meet the other deer and all the other animals! They will love you! I also have some human friends here at Nottingham and I would love for them to meet you too."

"That's wonderful! We would love to meet all of them," says Snowdeer.

So, Snowdeer introduces everyone to Buckingham and then Plum Puddin' says to him, "Our Magical Compass has broken. Do you know of anyone who can fix it?"

Buckingham replies, "My friend Traverman does watch repair and woodworking so I'm sure he could fix your compass. He and his son Austin have a repair shop in Coventry. I'm sure they would be happy to help you and would be good folks to know. Speaking of friends, before we go over to Traverman and Austin's, would you like to meet some of my friends and family?"

"Yes Sir, we would," answers Snowdeer.

Then Buckingham turns around to face the woods and says, "Ok, you can come out now."

"Yes Sir," voices reply from behind them and then to everyone's surprise, a group of other English Red Stag deer come out from the woods and walk up to them. They all seem to have a deep devotion to Buckingham.

"Thank you gentlemen," says Buckingham. Then he says to Snowdeer, "This is Caliber and his Deer Patrol," and then proceeds to introduce them.

After all the introductions have been made, Snowdeer, sensing that Buckingham is someone of great importance, asks him, "Who are you Mr. Buckingham, and what do you do, Sir?"

Buckingham replies, "I'm a public servant, and we travel all over England looking for whatever may be wrong so that we may make them right. I also bring along my fellow deer to assist me."

Then Snowdeer says, "Mr. Buckingham, I know beyond the shadow of a doubt that Santa meant for us to meet you and your Patrol. You were picked so that we could work with you in helping spread joy and cheer to your country, if you don't mind us doing so."

Buckingham laughs and answers, "Oh no, my good friend, you are just what England needs! We will be pleased to work with you!" Then Buckingham looks at the sun to see what time of day it is. Then he looks at the Magical Compass and then says to Snowdeer, "Let's go get that compass fixed!"

"Yes Sir!" answers Snowdeer, so all the gang and Buckingham, Caliber and the Deer Patrol start making their way to Traverman and Austin's repair shop.

33 - TRAVERMAN AND AUSTIN

As the gang heads toward Coventry, they notice people staring and whispering as they walk by. Snowdeer asks, "Mr. Buckingham, why are people acting like that?"

Buckingham answers, "They respect us because we take care of the people and the animals here in England. They stare at you because they don't know you yet, but they will."

Snowdeer looks at Plum Puddin' and Purple Mouse and then at Jim-Buck and Deerlores and makes his eyes big and shrugs his shoulders.

When they reach Coventry, Buckingham leads them to a little shop that's off to the side of the road in the country. The shop has a beautiful hand carved sign hanging out front that says, "Traverman & Son."

When they walk in, they find Traverman and Austin hard at work. Traverman is making rustic heart novelty candle holders out of wood and Austin is sawing a log into smaller pieces that will become candle holders. After Traverman and Austin have seen that they have entered, they immediately stop their work and come over and welcome the group.

Buckingham introduces everyone and Snowdeer tells Traverman and Austin about the Magical Compass that had broken. He tells them about their adventures with Santa and how they are there on special assignment from Santa to spread peace and good will to the people of England and everywhere else Santa sends them. Plum Puddin' and Purple Mouse tell their stories from the Knob Lick, Possum Holler and Doe Run days all the way up to their magical adventures with Santa and Snowdeer.

Traverman and Austin are thrilled to hear their stories and they immediately fix the Magical Compass. Snowdeer thanks them for working on it and Traverman says, "You are very welcome Snowdeer. Buckingham has us make special things for the King and Queen all the time and we are happy to assist you."

Austin says, "Anytime you are in England, please come by and see us and if we can be of service, please let us know."

Snowdeer, being very impressed with their friendliness and eagerness to fix the Magical Compass asks, "Traverman and Austin, would you like to come along with us? We are following the Compass and a Magical Map to see where Santa wants us to go." Then Snowdeer shows them the Magical Map and says, "If you would like to join us as our guests, we would be honored."

Traverman answers, "Thank You, I would enjoy coming along," and Austin says, "I would enjoy it too. Thank you for asking us Snowdeer. We don't meet folks like you every day and we want to be a part of your mission to help people and animals, so count us in."

Then Snowdeer says, "Great! It will be wonderful to have you both come along, but before we leave, what do we owe you gentlemen for your work on the Compass?"

Traverman answers, "You don't owe us anything. It is our pleasure to meet you and to get to travel with you, so we don't want any pay."

Austin says, "It will be payment enough for me just to see how the Magical Compass works.

Plum Puddin', who is holding the Compass, notices it starting to turn in circles. He motions for Traverman and Austin to quickly come over and take a look at the spinning Compass. They rush over and watch it spinning and spinning and then all of a sudden, it stops with its point showing southeast. Plum Puddin' then announces, "The Magical Compass is showing us that we need to head southeast."

Purple Mouse, who is holding the Magical Travel Map, gets curious to see if it has any new instructions, so he takes it from his pocket and opens it up to see. And just like the Compass, the Magical Map lights up and shows that they need to head southeast and go to the city of London. Purple Mouse excitedly shows everyone the Map and announces the Map's instructions.

Traverman and Austin ask to inspect the Map, and they are amazed at how it works! They pass it on to Caliber and the Deer Patrol who also are in awe of it!

Then, Buckingham also asks to see the Map, and after studying it, he is very impressed and he says, "We must do what it says, and be on our way."

34 - BUCKINGHAM PALACE

The gang follows Buckingham as he leads the way to London. Buckingham suddenly looks at Snowdeer and says, "Do you want to do some castle and palace sightseeing on the way?"

"Yes Sir!" answers Snowdeer.

So Buckingham leads the group down a well-groomed country lane by a river, where sits a beautiful castle.

"We've never been in a real castle before," Snowdeer admits.

Then Buckingham says, "Well my friend, this will be your first. And it is a beautiful one indeed! This is Warwick Castle. It's a medieval castle developed from an original built by William the Conqueror in 1068. The river we are standing by is the River Avon."

"What a beautiful castle and grounds," says Jim-Buck.

"Want to go in?" asks Buckingham.

" Could we? Oh, yes Sir," they all answer.

So, Buckingham goes up to the castle entrance. The guards, seeing him, immediately salute and let him and the entire gang enter. Snowdeer again thinks there is something really special about Buckingham, because of the way the people and animals alike treat him. After the tour of the castle, they all thank Buckingham.

Buckingham immediately asks, "If you enjoyed the Castle, would you like to see a real palace as well?"

"Really? Yes!" they all answer.

Buckingham says, "Alright, I'll take you there."

In a while they come upon a beautiful palace and Buckingham says, "We are near the town of Woodstock and this is the Blenheim Palace."

"Wow," says Snowdeer.

Buckingham asks, "Would you like to tour the inside?"

"Yes Sir," they all answer.

So Buckingham once again sees to it that they can take a tour, and just like at Warwick Castle, Buckingham is saluted and treated very special.

After the tour, when they are back outside of the palace and admiring the grounds, Plum Puddin' says to Buckingham, "England sure has some beautiful places. I hope Santa has us come back here to your country a lot."

Buckingham answers, "I am sure he will. You are welcome here anytime Mr. Puddin'."

They move on, and in a little while they arrive at London. They cross the London Bridge and come upon another beautiful palace. Then Buckingham smiles and announces, "Welcome to Buckingham Palace my friends!" Snowdeer, Plum Puddin', Purple Mouse and the other's mouths drop as they learn not only where they are, but who's palace it is! Snowdeer looks at Buckingham and starts to ask, when Buckingham stops him and says, "Yes, Snowdeer this is my palace. This is where I help the King and Queen as they rule. I have been made king of all the deer and the other animals in the whole country of England."

"Oh, then we should bow to you, your Royal Highness," says a shocked Snowdeer and so they all bow to Buckingham.

When they have finished bowing, Buckingham says, "There is much good that needs to be done here in London and actually all of England. You'll meet the King and Queen tonight and we'll talk about how we'll all work together to make our country stronger. But first, I want you to go to your rooms and rest and get ready to meet the King and Queen tonight." Then Buckingham asks Caliber and his Patrol to take Snowdeer, Plum Puddin', Purple Mouse and the gang to their rooms.

Snowdeer asks, "Sir, what about the sleigh and everything we left behind?"

Buckingham answers, "I will send the Red Stag Patrol to go get them."

"Thank you for everything Your Highness," says Snowdeer, Plum Puddin', Purple Mouse, Carrot and the rest.

So, Snowdeer and the others bathe and nervously wait to come before the King and Queen. In a short while, there's a knock on Snowdeer's door and it is Caliber asking them to follow him to meet the Royals. As they enter the Throne Hall, Snowdeer and the gang see the Royals sitting up at the front and then to the side of them they see King Buckingham and his Queen. Snowdeer gets a lump in his throat, and as they approach the throne area, they bow.

Buckingham walks over to the King and Queen and says, "Your Majesties, this is Snowdeer. He and his friends Plum Puddin', Purple Mouse, Carrot and the others have been sent on a mission from Santa to help spread peace and good will to our beloved England." Then Buckingham introduces everyone.

The King looks at the gang and smiles and joyfully says, "Welcome to England Snowdeer! Welcome, everyone! Buckingham has spoken highly of you. Tonight, the Queen and I would be pleased to have you join us in the Royal Banquet Hall where we will have a feast and discuss our plans together!" They all bow again and thank His Majesty and the Queen for their kindness.

Then, Buckingham takes them over to his and his wife's thrones, and he says to the Queen, "Doeretta, these are my new friends that I was telling you about." And then he introduces them to her one by one.

After the introductions, the Queen says, "It is a pleasure to meet you. We look forward to serving England with you."

Then Buckingham says, "Yes, indeed it will be a great pleasure! Now please, let us go to the Royal Banquet Hall."

So, Snowdeer and the gang follow the Royals to the Banquet Hall where a big feast is to be served.

While feasting, they discuss ways the gang can meet with those in the Kingdom. They find out what needs the King and Queen, and Buckingham and Doeretta can help with. The King tells them they are welcome to stay at the Palace anytime they are on their trips. He also tells them the next day he will be sending out a royal announcement to all of the people and animals in the Kingdom to gather at the front of the Palace the following day where he will then introduce Snowdeer and the gang. The gang excitedly accept the King's gracious offer.

So the next day a Royal Proclamation is made all over England stating that Snowdeer and his team have come from the North Pole to speak with them and deliver peace and good will on a mission from Santa. The following day, the day of the Event, the crowd is so thick that Snowdeer wonders if they can even open the Palace doors. After the trumpet sounds, Caliber and the Red Stag Patrol open the door and stand guard as the King and Queen with King Buckingham and Queen Doeretta behind them Snowdeer to the people.

Snowdeer can't believe he is in the presence of Royals and thousands of Englanders. He lowers his head and thanks God for this opportunity to do good in the world. Then, Snowdeer and the gang walk up and bow to honor the Royals and then turn around to face the crowd.

The King introduces Snowdeer, Plum Puddin' and Purple Mouse to his Kingdom, and then says, "Please welcome them to Buckingham Palace." The Kingdom gives them a mighty cheer and then the King continues, "Buckingham, King of the animals, found these travelers at Nottingham where they had just flown in from the North Pole on Snowdeer's own private sleigh on a special mission from Santa. They have been sent directly from him to our Country to bring peace and good will to us! They will be coming to visit us at different times throughout the year, not only at Christmas time. They will now walk down the steps to a platform where they will meet you, whether you are human or animal, and build a friendship and hear your concerns. They will then report back to us and we will help you. We look forward to building peace and good will with them and with Santa for ages to come. Please show your support by once again making Snowdeer and the North Pole team welcome!" Another great cheer comes over the crowd and the King motions for them to walk down the Palace stairs to greet the Kingdom.

After hours of meeting humans and animals and hearing of needs they have, Snowdeer and the gang are exhausted. Buckingham and Doeretta have stayed with them the whole time and have been asked by the King to meet with him once again in the Royal Banquet Hall to eat and to discuss the concerns of the day. Buckingham asks Caliber and the rest of the Red Stag Patrol to bring Snowdeer and the group once again to the Royal Banquet Hall. As the Patrol escorts them up the palace steps to the entrance of Buckingham Palace, Buckingham and Doeretta are waiting for them. They thank everyone for all the work they have done for England.

Snowdeer thanks them for the honor of getting to serve their Country and then Carrot says, "I'm so hungry I could eat a whole bushel of greens and carrots!" This causes the whole gang to laugh, including Buckingham and Queen Doeretta.

Then Buckingham says, "Then my dear rabbit, we had better get you over to the Banquet Hall before you pass out!" So, the Red Stag Patrol lead them to the great Hall to feast with both of the Kings and the Queens.

While they are eating, the King says to the gang, "Thank you very much for your work today. All of England thanks you."

Snowdeer answers, "Your Majesty, it is our honor. Thank you for having us and letting us serve."

Then the King asks, "How long will you be able to stay with us Snowdeer?"

Snowdeer answers, "Your Majesty, honestly, we don't know."

Then Plum Puddin' pulls the Magical Compass out of his pocket and shows it to the King and Queen and says, "Your Majesty, when Santa makes this Magical Compass spin 'round and 'round and then stops, that will let us know it is time to go toward wherever the Compass pointer has stopped."

Then Carrot pulls the Magical Map out and shows it to them and says, "When this Magical Map lights up, it will show us where we are to go next."

35 - THERE GOES THE COMPASS AGAIN

Just as Plum Puddin' says that, the Magical Compass starts to spin. They all marvel as the arrow quickly goes 'round and 'round and then stops, pointing to the southwest.

"Southwest," says Buckingham.

"Yes, Your Majesty," says Plum Puddin'.

"It looks like we'll be leaving in the morning," says Snowdeer.

"Do you know where you will be going?" asks Buckingham.

Purple Mouse gets out the Magical Map that is lit up and he says, "South America!"

"O, my dear," says Doeretta.

Then Carrot says, "We're gonna be flying a long way tomorrow."

Buckingham says, "We'll let you rest and see you in the morning. We will have a breakfast for you and send along a special goody bag of treats to take with you for your long trip."

"We deer know just exactly what to send with you," jokes Doeretta. They all laugh and then Doeretta realizes that Plum Puddin' and some others are not deer and she asks, "Plum Puddin', what do you like to eat the most?" The rest of the gang snickers because they know exactly what he will say to the Queen.

Plum Puddin' gets a big grin on his face and says, "Your Majesty, I love Plum Pudding the most. I eat it all the time whether I'm at Possum Holler there by Knob Lick or at the North Pole. My Mama Rose Marie or Mrs. Claus always makes sure I have it!"

"Then you shall have it in the morning," says Queen Doeretta.

"Thank you ma'am...oops....Your Majesty," replies a blushing Plum Puddin'.

Purple Mouse sees that Plum Puddin' is blushing, so he gets a mischievous look on his face and says to Plum Puddin', "Well, well, it looks like I'm not the only one who's known to blush!"

Everyone laughs except the King, Queen, Buckingham, Doeretta, Caliber and the Red Stag Deer Patrol, and it is only because they don't know about Purple Mouse's tendency to turn purple when blushing.

"What do you mean?" asks Doeretta.

Plum Puddin' then gets a mischievous look on his face and he wastes no time walking over to Queen Doeretta and whispers in her ear saying, "Say, "TASHA" to Purple Mouse and then watch his face." Purple Mouse sees what's happening and he starts thinking, "OH NO! HERE IT COMES!"

Without missing a beat, Queen Doeretta walks over to Purple Mouse and looks him square in the eyes and says, "TASHA!!!" Purple Mouse instantly turns a bright purple and Queen Doeretta, the King, Buckingham, Caliber and all laugh and laugh. Then Doeretta says, "You must really be blooming crazy about her!"

This makes Purple Mouse blush even a brighter purple and so he smiles, bows to the King and Queen and says, "I think I'm gonna call it a night!" and off he runs to his room, still blushing a bright purple.

They all laugh again and then say their good nights and Caliber and the Red Stag Patrol lead them to their rooms.

36 - SOUTH AMERICA, HERE WE COME!

The next morning bright and early, Snowdeer and the gang meet with the King and Queen and King Buckingham and Queen Doeretta for a grand breakfast before heading out for South America. For this special day, King Buckingham had even invited two of he and Doeretta's dearest friends, Tami Dunn, who makes the finest pastries in all England, and Kevin Dunn, who is a professor at Dunn College at Kensington, the college that had been named for the Dunns. They had come to Buckingham Palace early to make the pastries, and as they enter the room with their latest baked goodies, Buckingham introduces them to Snowdeer and the gang. Everyone is thrilled to meet them and they all thoroughly enjoy their fresh baked English delicacies.

Buckingham had also invited another great friend, Berry Wynn, the traveling singer and mandolin player, affectionately nicknamed Berwyn, to come and entertain them for this special event. Snowdeer enjoys them all so much that he invites Kevin, Tami and Berwyn to stay and watch their takeoff to South America. They answer saying they wouldn't miss it for the world.

Once breakfast is finished, and they are getting ready to leave, the King says to Snowdeer, "Thank you for visiting our Kingdom and for all you have done. Please come back soon. You will always have our friendship here in London, and indeed, in all of England."

The Queen also thanks them and says, "Please, give our regards to Santa and Mrs. Claus."

King Buckingham smiles and thanks them and gives each one a warm handshake.

Queen Doeretta thanks everyone and then takes a big picnic basket from one of the Red Stag Patrol deer that has been filled with goodies that Kevin and Tami Dunn had prepared, and she hands it to Purple Mouse.

She smiles at him and then not being able to resist, she says, "TASHA!" and everyone breaks out in laughter as Purple Mouse blushes a bright purple!

Then she takes another basket from another one of the Red Stag Patrol deer and walks over to Plum Puddin' and hands it to him. She smiles and says, "This is for you Plum Puddin'-your very own basket of Plum Pudding!"

Plum Puddin' is thrilled to receive such a great gift and he says, "Thank you very much Your Majesty. You couldn't have given me a better gift!"

They all laugh and Snowdeer says, "I look forward so much to coming back. Thank you everyone for your kindness, your Royal Highnesses. Caliber and all of you

Red Stag Deer Patrol, thank you! And thank you too Traverman and Austin for fixing the Magical Compass and to you Tami & Kevin for the pastries!"

Tami replies, "When you come back again Snowdeer, we'll make you all some more." Kevin says, "The next time you come, we'll give you a tour of our college!" Then, they thank Berwyn for singing and playing some songs during their breakfast. Berwyn replies, "Come back again Snowdeer, and I'll put you on a full concert!" They all thank Snowdeer and the gang for all they had done for England and then after they all say their goodbyes, they start walking toward Snowdeer's sleigh that has been placed on a long ramp lined with the Sugar Snow! Snowdeer looks at the Sugar Snow and says, "How I have missed you Sugar Snow!" The Sugar Snow flies up to Snowdeer and the gang and they tell them they have missed them too. Then they go back to their places lining the launching strip waiting for their orders.

By now, the news of them leaving had spread across London and a crowd has formed at the Palace to watch them take off. While Caliber and the Red Stag Deer Patrol assist in harnessing the deer to the sleigh, Snowdeer motions for some of the Sugar Snow to come over to him. After they do, Snowdeer whispers to them asking if they and the other Sugar Snow would please go up to the Royalty and to Caliber and the Red Stag Deer Patrol, Traverman, Austin, Kevin, Tami and Berwyn and thank them and then come back and give them and all of the Kingdom a Sugar Snow Light Show. The Sugar Snow immediately fly over to the other Sugar Snow and ask if they will do it and they all reply yes! Then, they fly over to Plum Puddin' and all the gang and whisper to them what they are going to do and they tell them what magic words to say to begin the light show. So after all are in their places, Snowdeer announces, "Your Royal Highnesses, thank you again for your kindness. God bless and keep you and your beloved England! Before we go, we have a gift we want to share with you." The Royalty and everyone in the Kingdom can't imagine what these ambassadors from the North Pole will do, nor are they prepared for what was coming! Then Snowdeer and all shout, "SUGAR SNOW! SUGAR SNOW! GIVE ENGLAND A GRAND LIGHT SHOW!" Immediately, the Sugar Snow starts flying through the air and over to the Royalty and they say to each one, "Thank you, Your Highness," and then they go to the others and thank them also. Then, they fly above all London and start putting on a grand light show–even though it is in the morning hours. The Sugar Snow is blessed with the ability to create such brilliant color, that no matter what time of day it is, they still shine! The morning is cloudy and dreary and the sun hasn't peeked through yet, so their color shows up in a great way that thrills all who are watching!

When the Sugar Snow Light Show has finished, Snowdeer and all the North Pole gang wave and say goodbye. The Sugar Snow swirls around the Royalty and their friends and then over to Snowdeer and all the gang and then lines the launching ramp getting ready to whoosh them off. Buckingham and Doeretta run down the stairs and Buckingham says, "I forgot to ask, where in South America are you going?" Snowdeer asks Purple Mouse to look at the Magical Map and after looking, Purple Mouse says, "It shows Chile!" Buckingham and Doeretta smile and Buckingham announces out loud to the whole Kingdom, "Snowdeer and the North Pole Gang are headed to South America to the country of Chile!"-which makes the whole Kingdom cheer! Plum Puddin' begins to feel something moving in his shirt pocket and he discovers it's the Magical Compass going off, so he pulls it out and sees it spinning wildly. After it stops spinning, he checks the direction on it and then he says, "The Compass stopped moving and is pointing southwest, so I guess we'd better go."

As Plum Puddin' is putting the Magical Compass back in his pocket, he sees Professor Kevin and his wife Tami rushing down the Palace steps toward them. After they reach the gang, Kevin and Tami ask them to explain the Magical Compass and Map. Plum Puddin' and Purple Mouse happily tell them the story of how Santa made it for them and Kevin says, "I'm going to start teaching about you all and Santa and the North Pole and your Magical Compass and Map to the students. They will no doubt be interested! Every time you come back, I would like to hear more about your travels, so I can document it all and then teach your traditions so they will be remembered and carried on to future generations!" Then Tami says, "Please know that any time you are here in London, I will be happy to bake more pastries for you. We also want you to see our college at Kensington!" "We would love that!" answers Snowdeer. Then Snowdeer gets a big grin on his face and starts laughing and Plum Puddin' asks, "What are you laughing about Snowdeer?" Snowdeer looks at Plum Puddin' and then at Kevin and Tami and answers, "I just got to thinkin', we have a Dunne's Christmas Buns Shop at the North Pole! I wonder if you are related to them?" Kevin and Tami's mouths drop open and Plum Puddin' says, "Well, I'll be! We'll need to take you all up there sometime! Even though the Dunne's at the North Pole have an "e" on the end of their name, you all might still be kin!" Kevin says, "We would love to go with you someday to the North Pole and see if we are related to them and also to meet Santa and Mrs. Claus!" Then Tami says, "Yes, we would love to go with you all up there! I'd love to meet them too and I'm curious to see if they make their pastries the same way we do!" "We will take you there for sure so you can find out!" says Snowdeer. Then all of a sudden, the Magical Compass starts going off again, reminding them that Santa is wanting them to head south. So, after they all say goodbye to Kevin and Tami, he looks around at Russ Elf and asks him to please turn on the Magical Music Box. Russ Elf is happy to oblige and as soon as the music starts, Snowdeer, Plum Puddin', Purple Mouse, Carrot and all wave at everyone and then say, "SUGAR SNOW! SUGAR SNOW! OFF TO SOUTH AMERICA GO!" So, the Sugar Snow, who had been lining the runway, fly up and around the passengers and the deer and then, Whoosh! Off they go on to their next destination!

37 - HOLA PUDDU

As the gang races through the air over England, Snowdeer happens to look below and then shouts, "Look! The London Bridge!" They all look down at the famous bridge full of people and then watch it until it gets so small they can't see it anymore.

In just a little bit, Plum Puddin' looks at the Magical Map and says, "We're going over the Atlantic Ocean now."

"And it looks like we will be for a long time according to the Magical Map," adds Purple Mouse, who had been looking at the Map with Plum Puddin'. So, for a few hours they fly below the clouds to enjoy the view of the great Atlantic Ocean and then they fly above the clouds to see the beautiful sun and clear skies. "God sure did great making this earth with all of its wonders, didn't He?" Purple Mouse says.

"Yes, He sure did," answers Russ Elf. Then Russ thinks of the Magical Music Box and asks, "Would anyone like to hear some music? We're going to be in South America soon and this will help us prepare for it."

"Yes! Please play us some music!" everyone shouts.

So, Russ Elf cranks the Magical Music Box and out comes a beautiful Spanish tune. As the tune is playing, they all glide through the air, loving the feel of the wind as it blows across them.

Jim-Buck says to Deerlores, "Santa has been enjoying flying like this for hundreds of years! We are so fortunate to be able to do this!"

"Yes, we sure are Jim-Buck, and I hope to do this many, many more times with Snowdeer," Deerlores replies.

Branson the Balladeer looks over at Dosi Doe and says, "I hope someday Daddy Reuben and Mama Mary will come along with us and ride with Snowdeer in his sleigh." Dosi Doe answers, "Oh yes, I sure hope so too! They have never seen anything like this in their lives and I know they would love it!"

Snowdeer's brother Deerell and sister Rosie look at each other and Deerell says, "We've come a long way from Doe Run, haven't we Rosie?"

Rosie answers, "Yes, we sure have Deerell. To be up here flying with Snowdeer and our Mama and Daddy and the rest of the family is something I never would have imagined!"

"Yeah, me either," Deerell replies.

Snowdeer's other brothers Longnose and Antler overhear what their sister and brother have said and Antler says, "Longnose, it's going to be a whole lot warmer down where we are headed. Do you think we will meet any other deer there? Do deer even live that far south?"

Longnose answers, "I don't know, but I am curious to find out. Hey, why don't we lay on the beach and get a tan while we're there?"

Antler laughs and says, "I don't know if you have noticed, but you already have a tan!"

Then Longnose jokes and says, "I know. I'm just kiddin' ya. But you know, I'd rather have my hide tanned just a little bit by the sun while laying on a beach, than having my hide tanned the other way!"

Antler laughs and shakes his head at his brother and then looks below and starts to see some shoreline. "Look below! Land!" Antler shouts.

"Yay!" the whole gang cheers.

Then Snowdeer asks Carrot, "Where are we now?"

Carrot looks at the Magical Map and Plum Puddin' grabs the Magical Compass. As he takes it out of his pocket, it begins to go 'round and 'round and then stops with its point heading southwest. The country of Brazil lights up on The Magical Map. Then Carrot tells everyone, "We're in Brazil." Then Carrot looks back down at the Map and after studying it awhile, he says, "South America is so big! We have a long way to go yet before we reach Chile!" In a little bit, Carrot announces, "The Magical Map is showing that next we will be going through Paraguay."

Snowdeer gets an idea and he calls out to the deer, "Would you fly closer to the ground please, so everyone can see the landscape better?"

The deer answer back, "Yes!" and downward they go.

As they get closer to the land, Purple Mouse says, "Look at the beautiful mountains! They're so close to the shore!"

"Yes, and see the palm trees along the trail of sand," says Russ Elf. "And look! There's a waterfall! Wait, there are four waterfalls together!" he counts.

"Pretty different from the North Pole or Possum Holler or Knob Lick!" Plum Puddin' jokes and laughs.

"Yeah, and quite different from Doe Run too, but I love it all," says Snowdeer. They all agree and just after Snowdeer says that, the Magical Compass starts spinning.

"I wonder why it's spinning now," asks Plum Puddin'.

Then Carrot looks at the Map and says, "It's because we are at a place called, "The Triple Frontier." It's where the countries of Brazil, Argentina and Paraguay meet."

"What a beautiful sight," says Snowdeer.

They soon cross over into Argentina and enjoy the sights of that country. Then, the Magical Compass spins again and points to the southwest.

Carrot checks the Magical Map and says, "We are now in the lowlands called, "The Pampas."

"Let's fly down closer so we can see more of what's going on," says Snowdeer.

So down they fly, and they find a very fertile lowland that spreads out as far as they can see. After getting a close look at the lay of the land and at some of its creatures, Snowdeer excitedly says, "Look! There are foxes, and so many birds! And look! There's a man herding sheep!

And there's even skunk down there!" Plum Puddin' laughs and says, "We gotta tell Snowcap 'bout that! I'm sure he'll want to come down here in the future with us!"

After a while, they start flying over water again and Carrot says, "According to the Map, we're flying over the South Atlantic Ocean."

Then shortly, Jim-Buck sees land again and announces, "Land everyone!"

The Magical Compass goes off again and Plum Puddin' looks at it as Carrot looks at the Magical Map and says, "We are at Cape Horn, in the very southern tip of Chile! Where we are at right now is where the Pacific and Atlantic Oceans meet."

The whole gang is in awe at the sight. The Magical Compass once again goes off and Carrot checks the Magical Map and says, "The Magical Map is lit up and showing we are to stay here."

"Yay!" the gang cheers and Snowdeer says, "Let's fly down and look around."

So, as they head toward the ground, they admire the mighty mountains as well as the miles and miles of coastal line. Snowdeer then says, "Let's look for a safe place to land that doesn't have any signs of life nearby." They eventually see an area that looks clear of people and has beautiful waterfalls, so they land there. "Look at the mountains," Snowdeer says.

"Yes, they are the Andes," a voice behind him says. Snowdeer looks around but doesn't see anyone. Matter of fact, nobody sees where the voice is coming from. "I'm over here," says the voice. Then a small deer walks through the grass and right up to them. "HOLA! Welcome to Chile!" he says. Startled at seeing such a small deer, they all back away. Laughing, the little deer says, "You surely aren't afraid of me! I'm the smallest kind of deer in the whole world!" They all laugh and Snowdeer and the gang walk up closer to him. Then the friendly little deer says, "My name is Puddu. It's really true that my kind of deer are the smallest."

Snowdeer smiles at him and says, "Hello Puddu, my name is Snowdeer and we are from the North Pole."

Puddu's eyes get real big and he says, "Please tell me once again, where are you from?"

Snowdeer repeats, "We're from the North Pole. Santa sent us to your country."

Puddu finds it hard to believe, but he puts a smile on his face and says, "Please stay and tell me all about yourselves. I want to meet every one of you and learn about you and the North Pole."

So Snowdeer starts introducing Plum Puddin', then Purple Mouse, Russ Elf, Carrot, and then his parents and the rest. Puddu gets so excited at meeting these new friends that he could jump! Which wouldn't be too high!

Then Snowdeer says, "Puddu, most of us are from the United States, way up in North America, but we spend time at the North Pole with Santa. It's a place where there is ice all the time at the very top of the world!"

Puddu shakes his head and says, "It gets so hot here that it is hard to believe somewhere else can be that cold, AND icy! How different than here where I live! These Andes Mountains are the longest mountain chain in the world. There are also some active volcanoes here too," Puddu tells them. Then he says, "And there is the Aconcagua Mountain that rises 22,831 feet and it's the highest point in the Americas."

"We'd better make sure we watch for that one on our way back north," Plum Puddin' says laughing.

Puddu laughs too and then asks, "So, why are you here?"

Snowdeer answers, "Puddu, I have a long story to tell you–if I may."

Puddu eagerly nods yes and Snowdeer tells him of his early days of his family at Doe Run and meeting Plum Puddin' and the trip to see Santa and having his Christmas Wish come true and then becoming Santa's Ambassador to spread peace and good will around the world. Puddu is so excited with Snowdeer's story that he asks, "Can I go with you to see Santa and the North Pole someday?"

Snowdeer answers, "You know Puddu, when I get back to Santa's, I will ask him. I would love to take you there with me."

Then Puddu excitedly says, "Now that I know why you are here, I want to introduce you to my dearest friends who live on the other side of the waterfall. His name is Dan and his wife is Malissa and their children are Alexander and Isabella. They are friends of the King and Queen. They are doing work for the King and Queen by going out as Ambassadors, not only for Chile, but for all of South America! They travel and bring peace and goodwill, just like you do! Dan is also a writer and documents their many trips. You've got to meet them!"

Snowdeer agrees and nods his head and says, "Yes, my friend, we would love to." Then Snowdeer looks around and notices the sleigh and wonders what he should do with it after they leave to meet Puddu's friends, so he asks Puddu,

"Where can we hide the sleigh?" Puddu answers, "I have an idea. Can we fly your sleigh to meet them?"

Snowdeer answers, "Why yes, we would be happy to take you in the sleigh! Let's all jump in. Now Puddu, would you please tell the Sugar Snow what direction to go?"

"Sugar Snow?" Puddu says.

"Yes, Sugar Snow," Snowdeer answers and then he explains how the Sugar Snow works. So, when everyone is in their places and ready for takeoff, Snowdeer tells Puddu and everyone the magic words to say. Then Snowdeer counts it off saying, 1...2...3..., "SUGAR SNOW! SUGAR SNOW! OFF TO PUDDU'S FRIENDS WE GO!" and the Sugar Snow circles the sleigh.

Some of the Sugar Snow tickle Puddu and then laugh and giggle with him as he gives them directions to get to his friends home. Puddu has the time of his life riding in Snowdeer's sleigh and giving them a personal tour of Chile while on their way to meet his friends. Russ Elf puts on beautiful music that's just fitting for Chile as they fly all over Cape Horn, giving Puddu a birds eye view of the native country that he loves!

After a little while, Puddu says to them, "We're about there." Then he says to the Sugar Snow, "Please fly directly over the top of the waterfall below, and then fly down to the bottom of it, and then over to the bottom of that mountain. There will be a cottage nestled in between that mountain and the stream where the water fall drops."

So, the Sugar Snow does as Puddu says, and they fly down the beautiful flowing waterfall, feeling the cool mist of the water. Then they look below by the mountain and see a small cottage sitting by the streaming river all by itself.

38 - DAN, MALISSA, ISABELLA & ALEXANDER

After Snowdeer and Puddu land the sleigh in an open area by the mountain stream, everyone jumps out and Plum Puddin' and Purple Mouse unhitch the deer. Then they start walking toward Puddu's friend's cottage. When they arrive, Puddu knocks on the door. The door opens and standing there is a friendly man who welcomes Puddu, Snowdeer and the gang. When he looks past them and sees the sleigh. he gets a puzzled look on his face.

Puddu smiles and says, "Dan, these people are on a mission from Santa Claus at the North Pole to come here to our country to spread peace and good will to the people of Chile! That is why they are traveling by sleigh."

Dan shakes his head, trying to take it all in, but then breaks into a big smile and says, "Ok, in that case, I understand! Welcome to Chile and to our home! Won't you please come in?"

Once everyone is inside, Dan introduces the gang to his wife Malissa, their daughter Isabella and their son Alexander. Snowdeer introduces all of the gang to them, and before long, he and Plum Puddin' and Purple Mouse are telling stories from their early days, and then about Santa granting Snowdeer's Christmas Wish, and on up to their present time of being Santa's Ambassadors.

Dan gets out his note pad and starts writing it all down. The family is amazed at their stories, and Dan says, "I know the King and Queen of Chile, and you've got to meet them and tell them everything you've told us!"

Puddu looks at Snowdeer and nods to him as if to say, "I knew he would want you to meet the King and Queen!"

Dan continues, "You can stay here at the cottage . . ." but suddenly stops talking when he realizes that there isn't enough room for everyone. He starts counting everybody in the group. When he is done counting, he laughs and says, "We can divide you up and part of you can stay in the cottage, and part of you can stay in the barn, and tomorrow we'll go see the King and Queen."

They all thank Dan and Malissa and the family for their hospitality and Malissa says, "I've just baked some fresh bread and I have fruit jellies and some raspberry juice if you would like." The gang thanks Malissa and takes her up on her offer. She invites them to sit outside on the ground by the river and then she goes inside the cottage to prepare a picnic for them.

While they are waiting, Isabella looks at Snowdeer, Plum Puddin' and Purple Mouse and says, "Would you tell our family some more stories please? We love hearing about you and Santa and the North Pole."

They all smile at Isabella and Snowdeer answers, "We would love to Isabella!" Then he grins at Plum Puddin' and Purple Mouse and says, "Between Plum Puddin', Purple Mouse and I, we have so many stories, we could talk for days!" The rest of the gang laugh and nod yes because they have heard them over and over again!

Then Alexander asks, "Snowdeer, when we go to see the King and Queen, can we ride in the sleigh with you?"

Snowdeer smiles and answers, "Yes, you sure can. And your mother and father can ride along too."

After Snowdeer says that, out of the cottage comes Dan and Malissa bringing picnic baskets loaded with all kinds of meats and goodies! They sit the baskets on blankets on the ground and after Dan gives a prayer of Thanks, the feast begins! After they start eating, Snowdeer starts telling more stories about Santa and the North Pole. Dan also tells stories from their lives and about the King and Queen and how they asked him and his family to be on assignment to travel and spread peace and good will throughout South America. Snowdeer, Plum Puddin' and all the gang are so amazed at their stories that they can't wait to meet the King and Queen and to set up a time to meet many of the people of Chile!

After eating, the rest of the gang begin telling their stories too, which makes the day pass so quickly, and before they know it, the sun is setting and the Chilean moon is rising above them. They all laugh at the fact that they have spent so much of the day and now into the night visiting, but they are happy because they know they have met some great new friends and will have some great new adventures!

39 - A KINGLY DAY AT CAPE HORN

The next morning, they awake to the sound of Isabella and Alexander shouting, "Get up! We're going to see the King and Queen today!" They all jump out of their beds to find Malissa already up and preparing a big breakfast, complete with their favorite breads and jellies. Again, Dan leads a prayer of thanks to God for the meal and asks Him for direction for the day. After all have said Amen, they start eating.

Then Dan says to Snowdeer, "Alexander told me that yesterday he asked you if we could ride in your sleigh, but I wonder if you have enough room for all of us?"

Snowdeer replies, "We won't have room for everyone, but the ones who won't fit In the sleigh can ride on the deer pulling the sleigh."

"That sounds like fun," says Dan laughing.

So, after breakfast, Snowdeer asks everyone to go to the sleigh and to get in their places so they can get ready for take-off. Dan, Malissa, Isabella, Alexander and Puddu get in the sleigh while Purple Mouse and Plum Puddin' harness up the deer. Then, Purple Mouse, Plum Puddin' and the ones who don't fit in the sleigh pick a deer they want to ride on and they hop on. Snowdeer asks the Sugar Snow to make them ready to take-off, so immediately the Sugar Snow circles all the gang and the sleigh. Dan, Malissa, Isabella and Alexander sit in awe as they watch the Sugar Snow do their magic.

Then Snowdeer asks, "Is everyone ready to go?"

All the gang shouts an excited, "Yes!", so Snowdeer tells everyone the magic words to say. Then he says, "Ok! Now! 1...2...3... "SUGAR SNOW! SUGAR SNOW! OFF TO THE KINGS PALACE GO!" and immediately the Sugar Snow takes them off in a mighty WHOOSH that leaves Dan, Malissa, Isabella and Alexander speechless!

Snowdeer asks Dan to direct them to the Kings Palace and Dan graciously accepts. They all happily move onward through the beautiful Chilean sky, and in a little bit, Dan points for them to fly down to a clearing that's surrounded by trees close to the Kings Palace. After they land and everyone gets out of the sleigh and Plum Puddin' unhitches the deer, they start walking toward the Palace. As they get closer, the Palace Guards notice them, and change to an alert position, uncertain of the strangers that approach. But, when they see Dan and the family are with them, they ease up and Dan goes up to them and tells them that all is well and that they are on business to meet the King and Queen. The Palace Guards immediately lets them pass.

As they enter the throne room, Puddu whispers, "Just be yourself. Tell them your story, and you'll be fine."

When they meet the King and Queen, they find them to be very kind hearted. At first the Royals find it hard to believe that Santa sent them all the way to Chile from the North Pole! But, when Snowdeer explains the whole story and Puddu tells them what Snowdeer is saying is absolutely true, the King and Queen believe them and they want to help.

The King tells them, "Please know that you have our support in bringing peace and good will to Chile. We welcome you with open arms." Then the King tells them he will make a proclamation for them to go meet in the front of the Palace to speak to the people and explain their mission.

Like the King and Queen of England, the King and Queen of Chile were impressed with them. The King made a royal proclamation the following day throughout all Chili for the people to come the next day to meet Snowdeer and the gang. The Royals are eager for their Kingdom to hear Snowdeer tell about Santa and the North Pole and how Santa would be having them come from time to time to bring peace and good will to their country.

Then the King says to Snowdeer and the gang, "Anytime you come to Chile, you are welcome to stay at the Palace as our guests. He then turns to his servants and says, "Please prepare a banquet for our special guests for tonight, but before that, take them to the special chambers where they will be staying." Snowdeer and all the gang thank the King and Queen and then look at each other with great excitement!

The King, seeing their excitement, gets an idea and he smiles and says to them, "Would you like to see around the Palace?"

Snowdeer and all answer, "Yes, Your Majesty!" and so the King then asks for more servants to come and go with him and the Queen to give Snowdeer and the gang a royal tour around the Palace before the evening Banquet.

40 - ROYAL PROCLAMATION DAY

The next day arrives, and Puddu meets Snowdeer and the gang at the Palace Hall for breakfast with the King and Queen. The King tells them he has already sent out the Royal Proclamation for the meeting with the people of Chile for the following day. The excited gang grins from ear to ear, and they thank His Highness and the Queen for the honor of serving them and their country.

The King smiles and nods his head and says, "You're welcome! It is an honor to have you. The Queen and I thank you for coming and blessing our country." Then he looks at Dan and says, "Why don't you take our friends around Cape Horn for a grand tour? I know they would enjoy it."

The King then looks at Snowdeer and the gang and asks, "Did you know Cape Horn is the southernmost point of land north of Antarctica?"

The gang all reply, "No, Your Majesty, we didn't know that."

Then Dan smiles at the King and replies, "Your Highness, I would be honored to take our friends out to tour your Kingdom." So, after breakfast, the gang spends the rest of the day sight-seeing and walking along the many miles of shoreline of Cape Horn.

The following day, Royal Proclamation Day, the King asks the gang to follow him and the Queen outside to a platform in front of the Palace where they will speak.

Thousands upon thousands of people and animals have come from all over Chile to hear them, with most of them having to come by boat to get there. The news had even spread into Argentina, with many Argentinians coming to listen too. Dan and Puddu, who were already well accepted in Chile, were asked by the King to interpret for those in the crowd who didn't understand English.

After the King and Queen have taken their places at the platform, His Majesty begins, "Welcome everyone! Thank you for coming today to hear our friends from the North Pole!" Then, the King tells the story of Snowdeer and about their mission from Santa to bring peace and good will to them. He turns toward Snowdeer and all the gang and asks them to say whatever is on their heart.

Snowdeer goes first, and he gives a wonderful talk. After Snowdeer speaks, each of the others have their turn to share with the people. After they have all spoken, everyone applauds, letting them know they are welcome among the Chilean people and animals.

The good hearted King then tells the people that Snowdeer is planning on coming back many, many times in the future, and then he jokes with them saying that everyone in the Kingdom had better be nice and not naughty if they want anything from Santa! This makes everyone laugh, and causes them to love Snowdeer and the gang even more! Then, His Majesty says, "Snowdeer and the North Pole gang will be walking down the Palace stairs to greet as many of you as they can." The crowd cheers again, and for many, many hours, the gang speaks with the people and animals, and they do just exactly what they promised they would do. They bring peace and good will to the great people of Chile.

41 - PUDDU'S SURPRISE

After a very successful day with the King and Queen, they all visit over dinner and then go to their chambers to go to sleep. The next morning, they are awakened by the Palace maids who let them know the King and Queen have invited them to a special luncheon at noon. When they meet them promptly at 12 o'clock, they sit down to a meal of stew and Pastel de Choclo (meat and corn pie) with olives and vegetables.

The King and Queen are very gracious, and they tell Snowdeer and the gang they will have everything ready for them whenever they are ready to leave. The runway ramp has been prepared and the whole Kingdom has been invited to come see them take-off. What a thrill it was for them to be treated with such special care! After lunch, they thank the King and Queen and Dan, Malissa, Isabella, Alexander & Puddu and tell them they will let Santa know of their kindness.

Snowdeer looks at Puddu and says, "I promise you, when I get back to the North Pole, I will ask Santa if we can bring you back with us on one of our trips."

Puddu thanks Snowdeer, but he has a very sad look on his face because he wants so much to go with them.

Snowdeer feels sorry for Puddu, so he takes Plum Puddin', Purple Mouse and Carrot aside and whispers to them asking, "What do you think? Would Santa mind if we went ahead and asked Puddu to come along with us now?" Before they can answer, Snowdeer takes Dan and the family aside and whispers, "Dan, I know you and your family are close to Puddu. Would you mind if we took him back to the North Pole with us for a little while?"

Then Dan whispers, "We would love for Puddu to go along with you. The King and Queen and my family are truly family to him down here, but, if I know Puddu, he will make many, many friends where ever he goes."

Plum Puddin' whispers, "I'm sure Santa would have no problem with us bringing Puddu back to the North Pole."

Snowdeer agrees and whispers to them, "Ok, then. It is decided. We will bring him with us." So, Snowdeer walks up to Puddu and puts a hoof on his shoulder and says, "Puddu, we all want you to come along with us to the North Pole today! We know Santa would love to have you! Would you please come?"

This makes Puddu so happy that he jumps in the air and shouts a loud, "Yes!"

Snowdeer laughs and says, "Then, Ok world traveler! You're now part of Santa's North Pole Kingdom Flyers! There's so much you are going to see on this adventure and the temperature is going to be way different than it is here! You will be glad you have a nice coat of hair on you!"

Everyone laughs and Puddu says, "It doesn't matter to me what the temperature is, just as long as I can be with you all! I look forward so much to flying to the North Pole with you and meeting Santa and Mrs. Santa and then to come back here to see the King and Queen and Dan, Malissa, Isabella and Alexander and tell them about our experiences!"

Then Snowdeer says, "That's great Puddu! We're so happy to have you on board with us! Now, the first thing we're gonna teach you is the magic words to say to the Sugar Snow when we need them to fly us to the North Pole." Puddu gets a big grin on his face as he waits to hear the magic words. Snowdeer then says, "Here they are.... "SUGAR SNOW! SUGAR SNOW! OFF TO THE NORTH POLE WE GO!"

An excited Puddu says, "Oh, Wow! I love it! I will always remember those magic words!"

Then, Snowdeer says to the Sugar Snow, "Please prepare for takeoff!" He then gets a big grin on his face as he gets an idea and he asks the Sugar Snow, "Would you please give us a Sugar Snow Light Show on our way out?"

The Sugar Snow raises up and flies over to Snowdeer and tells him they would love to do a Light Show, and for him to just give them the word.

After they all say goodbye to the King and Queen and Dan, Malissa, Isabella and Alexander, Snowdeer nudges Puddu and says to him and everyone else, "Ok, let's get ready for take-off! Everybody get in their places!" After everyone is in the sleigh, and the deer are harnessed, Snowdeer looks at Puddu and asks, "Would you lead us with the magic words please?"

Puddu answers, "With pleasure Snowdeer!" Then Puddu looks at everyone and says, "Ok, all together!" "SUGAR SNOW! SUGAR SNOW! OFF TO THE NORTH POLE WE GO!"

After they have said that, the Sugar Snow swirls around the sleigh and up and around Snowdeer, Plum Puddin' and all who are in the sleigh, and then around all the deer who are flying the sleigh. To honor the King and Queen, the Sugar Snow flies over to them, and while circling them, they thank them for everything. Next, they fly over to Dan, Malissa, Isabella and Alexander and circle them and thank them also. Then, right before taking off, the Sugar Snow once again circles Puddu. As they fly around him, they laugh and giggle and tell him they love him and that they are very happy he is now with the team. Then, as the gang waves goodbye, the Sugar Snow makes an extra swirl around them, and with a loud WHOOSH, off they go!

42 - MARKEY, KANTELOPE & EGYPT

Puddu can't keep the smile off his face as he's traveling with the gang.

Plum Puddin' notices it and says, "I think you are one happy deer my friend! We're so happy to have you with us!"

"I'm happy to be with you all too," answers Puddu. "I'm also happy because we're coming up to Mt. Aconcagua in Argentina. I have been wanting to come here for a long time."

Plum Puddin' scratches his head and says to Puddu joking, "Let's make sure we're powered up enough by the Sugar Snow so when we fly Snowdeer's sleigh over it. We don't want to bump it!"

Puddu laughs and Carrot says, "Puddu, would you like to learn about the Magical Map and the Magical Compass?"

"Yes sir!" answers Puddu.

Then, after taking the Compass out of his pocket and holding it up to Puddu, Carrot says, "Ok, here's the Magical Compass, and when it wants to tell us what direction Santa wants us to go, it will move in circles and then stop with the point headed in the direction Santa wants us to take."

Then, Purple Mouse gets out the Magical Map and after laying it out in front of Puddu he says, "The Magical Map will light up and show us where in the world Santa wants us to go. We also have a Magical Travel Log that we write in to keep track of where we have been so we can show Santa after we get back to the North Pole. Santa has a big library down in his underground lair and this is where he keeps his Magical Travel Logs. He has an amazing showcase down there in his lair and the best chocolate chip cookies and cocoa too!"

The gang laughs and then Russ Elf says, "Santa put me in charge of the Magical Music Box. Just tell me what music you want to hear and I'll crank it up for you."

They all laugh again and Puddu thanks Russ Elf and then says, "Thank you all for teaching me, because I want to learn all I can."

Carrot replies, "You are sure welcome Puddu. We are happy to help you in any way we can." Then Carrot breaks into a smile and says to Puddu, "I have to tell you Puddu, that Santa and Mrs. Santa are gonna love you."

Puddu replies, "I feel somehow that they already do because I feel drawn to them. Does that sound strange?"

"No, not at all," Snowdeer answers. Snowdeer says that to Puddu because he already knows Santa is drawing Puddu to visit them and that Santa has a purpose for him to fulfill. Then Snowdeer says to Puddu, "I wouldn't be surprised if Santa and Mrs. Santa have you stay a long time with them and give you lots and lots of milk and cookies. They'll probably talk with you for hours by their nice warm fire."

"Really?" asks Puddu.

"Yes, I really do believe that," Snowdeer answers. Then all of a sudden, the Magical Compass starts going around in circles!

Puddu says, "The Compass! It's going off!" Then, just as fast as it started, it stops!

Plum Puddin' looks at it and says, "It's showing northeast. It looks like Santa isn't ready for us to come home yet." Then he turns to Purple Mouse and Carrot and asks them, "Would you please look at the Magical Map and tell us where Santa wants us to go?"

Carrot opens the map and he and Purple Mouse scan it and then Carrot says, "We're going to Egypt!"

Everyone cheers and Puddu says, "Wow, my first time out of South America, and now I'm going all the way to Egypt! It's hard to believe!"

"Yes, I agree, it is hard to believe! It's our first time too, Puddu," says Purple Mouse. Then he turns to Russ Elf and asks, "Russ Elf, would you please play something on the Magical Music Box?"

"Yes sir!" answers Russ Elf, and he immediately starts cranking the box and beautiful Latin music comes out of it and fills the air.

"Hey, I know that song," says Puddu.

Then Snowdeer grins and says, "That's great Puddu. Please sing it for us, but if you dance, don't dance too hard 'cause we don't want you to blow out of the sleigh!"

Puddu laughs and then goes into the song singing and swaying instead of dancing.

The Magical Compass goes off again and it keeps pointing toward the northeast. Purple Mouse looks at the Magical Map and says, "It's showing that we are already halfway across Argentina!"

"What? We're flying that fast?" asks Puddu.

"Yes, the Sugar Snow takes their flyin' seriously!" answers Snowdeer, laughing.

In a short while, the Magical Compass starts spinning again and the Magical Map shows they are entering Bolivia. Then, around 30 minutes later, they fly into Brazil.

After Carrot announces it, Puddu says, "I never dreamed that anybody or anything could fly like this!"

Plum Puddin' leans over and asks Snowdeer if they could fly closer to the ground so that everyone could see some of the landscape up close. Snowdeer calls out to the deer to head downward so they can get a better look, and they happily do it. Puddu and the gang see mountain after mountain with beautiful waterfalls flowing through many of them. After a while, the Magical Compass goes off again and the Magical Map shows they are entering Venezuela and then soon to the Atlantic Ocean! Snowdeer relays this message to the deer and they get excited knowing that the scenery will soon be changing and within hours they will be in Egypt!

Snowdeer looks at Puddu and says, "Puddu, Venezuela is the last country you will see before we start crossing the Atlantic Ocean."

Puddu excitedly says, "It will seem so different being on the Atlantic Ocean north of South America instead of at the tip of South America where I'm from!"

Very shortly, the Magical Compass starts spinning wildly and then stops and again points northeast. As Purple Mouse starts to get the Magical Map, he hears Plum Puddin' say, "Ocean ahead." Everyone's mouths drop as they watch the land quickly pass behind them as they start flying over the big mass of blue that is the Atlantic Ocean! The Sugar Snow wants to make sure they are keeping the sleigh and everyone safe and at a great speed, so they start circling the gang and the sleigh to give them more power and WHOOSH! Off they go speeding across the Atlantic!

After several hours, Puddu says, "I've never seen so much water in my life! Where I am from there in Chili I see a lot of water because it is a coastal country and I've seen where the Atlantic and Pacific Oceans meet, but I've never been out this far in either ocean. It just keeps going and going!"

"Yes, it is amazing," agrees Carrot. "In the Ozarks where I'm from, I never saw an ocean, only creeks, rivers, lakes, ponds and water holes."

"It's sure strange to not see any land in sight," says Plum Puddin'.

Then Snowdeer looks at Plum Puddin' and says laughing, "It wouldn't be a good time for the Sugar Snow to run out and leave us behind, would it Plum."

Plum Puddin' gets a funny look on his face and says, "That's for sure!"

Snowdeer and Plum Puddin' didn't know it, but some of the Sugar Snow heard what Snowdeer said and they get together and decide to play a joke on them. So, some of the Sugar Snow get behind the sleigh and push a little bit downward, just enough to make them feel like they are falling. The gang in the sleigh gasps! The Sugar Snow who did it come up behind them and tell them it was just them, playing a joke.

A relieved Snowdeer laughs and says, "You must have heard what I said, but, I can tell you one thing, you'll never hear me say anything like that again!"

They all laugh and Russ Elf says, "May I suggest some music to change the mood?" They all say yes, so Russ Elf says something to the Magical Music Box and then starts cranking it, and it starts playing a beautiful song about the Sea. They all fall in love with it and begin swaying to the tune. Jim-Buck, Deerlores, Deerell, Rosie and all the deer who are pulling the sleigh love the melody too, and they smile at each other and pick up their pace as they listen.

After the song is over, they notice there are some low hanging clouds drifting their way. Then it starts sprinkling rain and Snowdeer is afraid it will become a big storm. He decides to instruct the deer to fly upward and above the clouds. As they go higher in the sky above, they find the beautiful sun and see fluffy blankets of clouds below.

"Wow, I feel like I'm in Heaven," says Carrot.

All of a sudden, the Magical Compass goes off again and shows them to continue northeast, but to go more east than they had been going before. Carrot relays that to Snowdeer who in turn relays it to the deer. By now, there is no rain below, and Snowdeer asks them to go back down through the clouds so they can see what lies below. As they fly below the clouds, the Magical Compass spins once more and they see land below!

Carrot looks at the Magical Map and after seeing where they are, he says, "The Map shows we are in Africa and in the country of Nigeria!" The whole gang is excited by the news and the Sugar Snow again flies around the sleigh and all the gang and off they speed with renewed power!

In a little bit, Carrot looks at the Magical Map and says, "Next is the country of Chad."

"We're really covering these countries fast," says Plum Puddin'. After they pass through Chad, they enter Libya and Snowdeer asks the deer to fly close to the ground so they can see what the lay of the land was like and what animals were there. Then, in what seemed only a short time, the Magical Compass starts spinning and showing them to continue heading northeast. Purple Mouse looks at the Magical Map and discovers they are in Egypt.

Then Purple Mouse tells them, "According to the Map, we're at Cairo, Egypt and the Map has Cairo lit up, so I think Santa is telling us to stop here." Snowdeer agrees, so they fly downward and close to the ground to look for a flat secluded place to land.

Russ Elf spots a place and tells them, "Over there to the right looks like a perfect place." They all agree and over to the spot they go.

After they have landed and everyone has jumped out of the sleigh, and the deer have been unharnessed, Snowdeer asks, "I wonder where there's any water?"

"It's over on the other side of the trees," a voice behind him answers.

"What?" a startled Snowdeer asks.

Then suddenly a monkey and an antelope come out from behind a tree and the monkey says, "Hello, my name is Markey and this is my friend Kantelope. Welcome to Egypt!"

"Thank you very much," answers a very surprised Snowdeer.

Then Markey says, "We want to meet your group. Please follow us to the water and tell us who you are as we go."

"Ok," answers Snowdeer. So, one by one the gang tells their names and where they are from. After everyone has been introduced, Snowdeer tells Markey and Kantelope about their mission from Santa and that he wanted them to stop there in Cairo.

Markey and Kantelope are thrilled to have them come to visit and Kantelope says, "Thank you for coming! We need you here to spread peace and goodwill! We are friends with the King and Queen, and we will take you to them so they can meet you and hear of your mission."

So, they go meet the King and Queen of Egypt and some of the other leaders of their country that very day. The King and Queen are very gracious, and just like in England and South America, Snowdeer tells them about Santa's mission for them to spread peace and good will to their country. Snowdeer also tells them he will be coming back from time to time, and not just at Christmas! The King and Queen and leaders are pleased with them and the King offers them food and lodging for the night. They gladly accept the King's offer, and they're treated like royalty. The King tells them that the next day he will make a public announcement for a great meeting in Cairo at his Palace. Snowdeer and all the gang will speak to and meet people and animals of the Kingdom the following day.

So, the next day, while the word is getting out to all the city, Markey and Kantelope show Snowdeer and the gang around Cairo, which is the capital of Egypt and the largest city in Africa. They see the Nile River and then they go over to Giza where they see the Great Sphinx and other sites from the ancient days of Egypt. Markey and Kantelope take them to see the camels, and Plum Puddin', Russ Elf and Purple Mouse each ride on one of them and take a trip to see the pyramids.

Markey warns them ahead of time saying, "Don't do anything to make them angry because they can spit."

Plum Puddin' laughs and says, "Surely they wouldn't do that.....," and SPLAT! a camel had looked around at Plum Puddin' and spit on him, hitting him directly in the face! "OOOOHHHH," is all Plum Puddin' can say, and Markey starts laughing and rolling on the ground, hitting it with his arms and legs!

Later that day, Markey asks Plum Puddin', "Plum, after hearing so much about Santa and the North Pole, could I come along with you on one of your trips someday?"

Plum Puddin' smiles and answers, "I'll ask Santa when I get home. Personally, I would love for you to come visit. Santa and Mrs. Santa would love you, and there's so much to see and do there, and there's gobs and gobs of elves! I know everyone there would love you!"

"Then it's a done deal Markey, you're coming with us on this trip," says Snowdeer, who had heard their conversation. Then Snowdeer looks at Kantelope and asks, "Kantelope, would you like to come to the North Pole too?"

Kantelope replies, "Oh, I would love to Snowdeer, but I can't leave my family. I am needed here in Cairo, but thank you very very much for your offer."

"That is perfectly fine Kantelope. Perhaps someday you will be free to go and when that day comes, you will still have an invitation to come visit us," says Snowdeer.

The following day, the King and Queen have their meeting with the Kingdom with Snowdeer and the gang, and it is a big success! Thousands upon thousands of people and animals come, and once again Snowdeer and the gang of ambassadors speak to the Kingdom. Then, they visit with the people and the animals, and they answer questions about Santa and the North Pole, and spread love and good cheer to all who are there.

The next morning, after everyone has had their breakfast with the King and Queen, they tell them goodbye and head to the sleigh to take off. As they get to the sleigh, Plum Puddin' hears the Magical Compass start to spin and he checks it. It keeps spinning and spinning and when it stops, it shows northeast. Purple Mouse quickly checks the Magical Map and it shows the country of Israel! Snowdeer, Plum Puddin' and the gang are thrilled to find out where they are going next! Purple Mouse explains to Markey how the Magical Map works and Carrot tells Markey how the Magical Compass and the Magical Travel Log works. Plum Puddin' tells Markey about the Sugar Snow and then teaches him the magic words that will make them fly.

"Ok," I think I understand it all," says Markey. Then after looking at the sleigh and the deer who are going to pull the sleigh, he asks, "Would it be alright if I ride on the deer sometime?"

"Why sure Markey," answers Snowdeer.

So, after all the deer are harnessed and the sleigh is loaded, Snowdeer asks the Sugar Snow if they are ready.

The Sugar Snow rises up once again, and they fly over to Snowdeer and say to him, "Yes Sir! We are ready! Just say the word and we're out of here!"

Snowdeer laughs, and then all of a sudden, he gets an idea, and he says to Markey, "Would you like to help us with the magical words to send us off please?"

Markey replies, "Yes! I would be honored to Snowdeer!" So, in true monkey fashion, after being told what to say by Snowdeer, Markey stands at the very back of the sleigh at the highest point, and while beating his chest, he leads the gang whooping and screeching, "SUGAR SNOW! SUGAR SNOW! OFF TO ISRAEL WE GO!" and WHOOSH! off they go to their next destination!

43 - MARKEY'S MONKEY BUSINESS

The Sugar Snow circles them from one end of the sleigh and the deer to the other! As a matter of fact, the Sugar Snow coated sleigh is going so fast, it causes Markey to blow out the back of it! But just in time, he grabs ahold of the back of the sleigh and hangs on for dear life, with his legs blowing in the wind! Russ Elf rushes to his rescue. He leans over, gives him his hand and pulls Markey back into the sleigh. Markey thanks Russ Elf for saving him and then to everyone's surprise, Markey takes a big leap from the back of the sleigh to the front of it and then jumps off the front and lands on the back of Branson The Balladeer! They all laugh and when Markey sees that they are amused, he jumps over to Dosi Doe's back! Then, one by one, he jumps up onto Antler's back and then onto the back of Longnose, who is right beside him. And with another big leap, he jumps forward to Deerell's back and then over to Rosie's back! He takes yet another big leap and jumps onto Deerlores' back and then over to Jim-Buck's back! After Markey lands on Jim-Buck's back, he beats his chest and gives out a big, "Whoop Whoop".

Jim-Buck looks at him, gets a big grin on his face and says, "If I had a banana, I'd give it to you for a prize!" This make everyone bust out in laughter and Markey goes into a dance on Jim-Buck's back and then starts climbing all over him!

After Markey settles down, he says, "What a view! This is higher than any tree I have ever climbed! How I wish my sisters Chatter and Gibber and my brothers Whoop and Screech could be here!" After staying up there for a while, Markey says, "I'm gonna jump back to the sleigh now-but I'll be back! Thank you all for the ride!" But, before he goes, he looks at Jim-Buck and says, "I'll be expecting that prize banana when we get to the North Pole!"

Jim-Buck grins and answers, "Good luck with that, my furry friend, I think the North Pole is plum out of them!" Everyone laughs and then Markey realizes they don't grow bananas at the North Pole!

He laughs and says, "Ok, you're off the hook Buck Daddy!" and then he jumps over onto Deerlores' back. Then he jumps on the harness that is connecting the deer and starts swinging on it. He takes off again and jumps onto Deerell's back, and then over to Rosie, and then goes all the way back to Branson The Balladeer. He jumps up and down on Branson's back and gives a big, "Whoop Whoop!" and then tickles Branson's nose and makes him sneeze! It brings so much joy having Markey along for the ride! Then they watch as Markey looks over and sees Dosi Doe and then gets a mischievous look on his face that lets Dosi Doe know he's up to something!

He suddenly jumps on her back and acts like he's galloping on a horse! Then, he reaches up and cups his hands over her eyes! Dosi Doe almost stops moving her feet to fly because she's laughing so hard and Snowdeer gets so tickled that he almost let's go of the reins! Then, Markey leans forward and looks Dosi Doe right in the eyes and smiles at her and then leaps back into the sleigh.

Snowdeer looks at Markey and laughs and says, "Great work my friend! You need to move to the North Pole and "Hang" with us all the time!"

Markey laughs and answers back, "I might do that, but I'm liable to drive you all ape with my monkey business!"

Snowdeer laughs and replies, "We can always use some monkey business at the North Pole! I'm sure Santa would love it!" Then Snowdeer and everyone in the sleigh start moving their arms up and down at their sides and saying, "Whoop Whoop, Ah, Ah, Ah!" and then bust out laughing!

The Sugar Snow sees everyone having a great time, and they decide they will have some fun too, so they start putting on a Sugar Snow Light Show! They swirl around everyone in a variety of colors that shows up boldly, even in the daytime, and they spell, "Whoop Whoop" and "Ah, Ah, Ah" and make shapes like monkeys! This makes everyone laugh and make monkey sounds. Markey starts once again going from one deer to the other and beating his chest and going, "Whoop Whoop! Ah, Ah, Ah!" When they come to the end of the Sugar Snow Light Show, the Sugar Snow circles everyone, giving them an extra boost of power, and then, WHOOSH! off they go with great speed through the sky on their way to Israel!

44 - ISRAEL

All of a sudden, the Magical Compass starts spinning, and the Magical Map shows they are off the coast of the Mediterranean Sea near Israel. When the Magical Compass stops spinning, it shows them that they should head northeast.

As they fly in that direction, Plum Puddin' says, "This is Israel, The Holy Land. It's a land I have read about many times in the Bible. This is the special land where my Lord and Savior Jesus Christ was born hundreds and hundreds of years ago."

This makes Purple Mouse very interested in where they will be going, so he takes out the Magical Map and looks at it. After studying it, he says, "The Map shows we are to head toward Bethlehem."

Snowdeer answers, "Ok," and then he instructs the deer to go northeast toward Bethlehem.

Plum Puddin' had more to say about The Holy Land, so he continues his story, "Jesus' parents were Joseph and Mary and she conceived Jesus by God's Holy Spirit. After Jesus was born in Bethlehem, they moved to Nazareth where He was raised." Plum Puddin' goes on to tell how Jesus become a carpenter, like His earthly father Joseph, and later became a preacher and shared His Heavenly Father's Gospel with thousands upon thousands of people. Plum Puddin' then tells them that many people turned their backs on Jesus and then, Jesus was whipped and crucified on a cross for the sins of all mankind. Plum Puddin' said Jesus did this so that if we turn from sin and ask Jesus to come inside our hearts, to be our Lord and Savior, He would. We would then be saved and when we die, we will go to Heaven.

"How great Jesus is!" Snowdeer says.

"Yes, He is," Plum Puddin' agrees. And then Plum Puddin' says, "Jesus died on a cross there at Jerusalem and was buried in a tomb. But then three days later, he was raised back to life again by His Father God! All we have to do is ask Him to come inside and to save us."

"Wow, a risen Savior," Purple Mouse says.

"Yes, for sure," answers Plum Puddin'.

"This is what you were talking to me about at my house!" says Carrot excitedly.

"Yes, it is my friend," answers Plum Puddin'.

The Magical Compass needle starts turning around again and then stops, still pointing to the northeast. Carrot checks the Magical Map and it shows they are arriving at Bethlehem. Markey checks the Magical Travel Log and finds there a special note from Santa telling them they are to land there. So, he tells Snowdeer, who in turn tells the team to start heading downward to land.

As they get closer to the ground, they notice a shepherds field and they see shepherds tending to their flocks. When the shepherds see the sleigh coming down with the deer, they quickly lead their flocks away from them. A beautiful Persian deer who sees them, runs up to them unafraid and says, "Shalom!"

Snowdeer, realizing that this is a Jewish greeting, repeats back, "Shalom!"

The deer then says, "Welcome to Israel, the land of the deer. My name is Fallo Tzvi."

Snowdeer answers, "It's a pleasure to meet you Fallo. I'm so thankful you know how to speak English, 'cause none of us know Hebrew!"

Fallo laughs and then asks, "What are you doing in the Holy Land? What is this flying thing you are riding in, and how do you make the deer fly? This is so meshuga!"

Snowdeer and Plum Puddin' look at each other and laugh, and then Snowdeer says, "Forgive me Fallo, but what does "meshuga" mean sir?"

Fallo answers, "It is Hebrew for, crazy!"

That makes everyone laugh and Plum Puddin' nods in agreement and says, "I think our new friend has us pegged early on!"

Everyone laughs again and then the gang begins to tell their stories of how they met and about the Knob Lick and Doe Run days. They tell Fallo about Reuben and Mary Branson, Santa and the North Pole, and about their special mission from Santa.

Fallo is thrilled to hear their stories and he says, "My family will be so happy to meet you! Please come with me and I'll introduce you to them!"

So, off they go to meet Fallo's family. When they get to Fallo's home, Fallo goes up to the door and sticks his head in and tells them he has company. But, what a surprise it is when they see who comes to the door! It's a Jewish human couple! Fallo tells them about Snowdeer and their Mission to bring peace and good will to Israel. After hearing that, they rush out the door to greet them!

"Shalom!" they both say. Then, the man says, "I am Hirsh and this is my wife Tzivia." When he sees Snowdeer and the gang's expressions, he laughs and says, "I can tell by your faces that you are wondering about Fallo and why his parents are human. We found him when he was very young. We couldn't find his parents, so we took him in and cared for him."

"We love him as our own," says Tzivia.

Branson The Balladeer and Dosi Doe look at each other and smile because Reuben and Mary Branson had taken them in and cared for them when they were young too.

Then Hirsh says, "Come in! Come in! We'll talk some more!"

"Thank you sir," says Snowdeer.

"Let me fix you something to eat," says Tzivia.

The gang thanks her for her kindness and they go inside.

After they are settled in, Snowdeer asks them, "Would you please help us meet people and spread peace and good will to the city of Bethlehem and to Jerusalem and to all of Israel?"

Hirsh answers, "Yes, we will be happy to help you all we can. We strive to have peace in our country and I know your country wants us to have peace also."

Tzivia says, "Please, stay with us while you are here. We will feed you and give you lodging and have you meet many of our friends."

"Thank you very much," say Snowdeer and Plum Puddin'.

Tzivia prepares them a great Jewish meal of meatballs, sweet potatoes, pita bread and a wonderful desert of different kinds of pastries. They enjoy this time together so much while they share stories from their different cultures.

Hirsh says, "Tomorrow we will introduce you to Linda & Sandi. They are friends of ours who live down the road from each other. I know they will take you in, just like we have."

Then Fallo says, "At Sandi's house, she has a beautiful young doe that lives with her and her name is Susan."

"We would love to meet them," says Snowdeer. So, they spend the rest of the day visiting and eating and enjoying each other's company.

The next day, Hirsh, Tzivia and Fallo take Snowdeer and the gang to see Linda, Sandi and Susan. When they arrive at Sandi's home, they find that Linda is there visiting. The two Jewish ladies and Susan answer the door, and when they see who it is, they hug Hirsh, Tzivia and Fallo, but they look at Snowdeer and the gang a little funny.

Hirsh sees their looks, and he immediately introduces them and begins to tell a little about them and about the Mission from Santa they are on.

After Hirsh explains this to them, Linda, Sandi and Susan immediately break into smiles and begin to hug them saying, "Thank you for coming! Please! Come in! Come in!" So, they all go in and visit for hours.

They trade stories just like they did when they were at Hirsh's house. Linda says to them, "I would be happy to take you to meet some of my friends! I want to help you spread peace and good will to others here in Israel!"

Sandi then says, "I also want to help you and I want to take you around to see our beautiful city and have you eat some of our Jewish food!"

Susan also wants to help and she says, "I will help you anyway I can to promote peace and good will between Israel and The North Pole! It is such an honor to meet other humans and other deer. In Hebrew the name for deer is Tzvi and the prophets of old used the word Tzvi to describe the Holy Land as "The Land of the Deer.""

"That's fascinating Susan," says Snowdeer and all the others agree.

Then Susan continues, "Fallo and I are great friends, and we have talked many, many times about us being deer and what our kind means to Israel. We want to stand for God with dignity and respect and want to bring peace and joy to our country, just like you do."

"You can be assured that we are on your side," says Snowdeer.

Then Susan asks, "Did you know that God's Holy Word says that whoever blesses Jerusalem will be blessed and whoever curses Jerusalem will be cursed?"

Snowdeer answers, "Yes, I knew that, and I always want to bless Israel."

"Me too!" Plum Puddin' says in agreement.

"Then you will be blessed," says Susan.

Sandi walks up to Linda and Susan and says, "Speaking of Jerusalem, why don't we take a trip over there now with our new friends?"

"Yes, that's a great idea!" answers Linda.

Susan says, "It has been awhile since I have been, and I would love to give a tour of The Holy City!"

Then Snowdeer gets an idea and asks them if they would like to take a sleigh ride to Jerusalem. They all get excited and everyone says, "Yes!" so Snowdeer says, "Let's go get ready and the Sugar Snow will take us there."

"Sugar Snow?" asks Linda.

"Yes," answers Snowdeer and then he explains how the Sugar Snow works.

All their new friends are very excited to take this trip to Jerusalem!

When they arrive at the sleigh, Snowdeer harnesses the deer and they load up the sleigh and whoever doesn't fit in the sleigh gets to ride on the flying deer.

Plum Puddin' tells the new riders the magic words to say, and then he says, "All together now!"

Then they all say the magic words, "SUGAR SNOW! SUGAR SNOW! OFF TO JERUSALEM WE GO!"

The Sugar Snow rises up and swirls around all the gang and WHOOSH! Off they go on their adventure to Jerusalem!

45 - JERUSALEM

As the gang arrives at Jerusalem, Snowdeer asks Fallo if he would lead them to a quiet place to land the sleigh. Fallo happily directs them to a perfect spot, and Snowdeer makes a safe landing. After they get out of the sleigh and the deer are unhitched, Snowdeer says, "It's hard to believe we're in The Holy Land!"

Susan laughs and says, "Well, you can believe it, and you're gonna love it!"

Fallo agrees and says, "You're in a wonderful, sacred city that has touched many millions of people and animals. I'm very thankful to live in this country!"

As they start looking around, they notice a couple coming up over a hill, and each one is riding a camel.

"Here comes Shalome and Jewel!" says Hirsh.

When the couple see the gang, they quickly stop and stare at the odd sight - all the deer and the humans and the sleigh! Hirsh, Tzivia, Linda and Sandi go over to Shalome and Jewel and greet them and know they have some explaining to do!

"Shalom," they all say to each other.

Susan walks up behind them and says, "Shalom, Shalome!" and then they all laugh.

They immediately start telling Shalome and Jewel about their new friends and the Mission from Santa. Shalome and Jewel get excited about Snowdeer and the gang, and they quickly climb off their camels and rush over to greet them! They immediately start sharing stories about each other, just like the others did when they met them.

After a while, Shalome says to everyone, "Let's walk inside Jerusalem and have some pomegranate juice and we'll show you around." They reach the city wall of Jerusalem and the Damascus Gate.

"I read about this gate in the Bible," Plum Puddin' says.

They walk through it, and even though they get some funny looks, especially at Carrot and Purple Mouse, they keep walking.

"The people here are not used to seeing a mouse and a rabbit dressed and walking on two legs," says Tzivia laughing.

"Yes, I am sure that is true," answers Purple Mouse and then he blushes his purple color.

"What is that?" asks Shalome.

Plum Puddin' laughs and tells them why Purple Mouse blushes like that. Then Plum looks at Purple Mouse and says, "Hey, I thought you only blushed for Tasha!"

Purple Mouse blushes even more and the new friends just stare at him and then break out in laughter. "I think it's time for some pomegranate juice," Purple Mouse says trying to change the subject and that makes them all laugh again. Shalome smiles and waves his hand for them to follow him to the place where they can have their juice.

Afterward, they walk the ancient city and take turns telling Snowdeer and the gang about the special sights. They walk up steps that go by an old church and Linda says, "Jesus walked on these steps and did a lot of great things and brought the country of Israel a lot of peace. As a matter of fact, Jesus is called, "The Prince of Peace."

Plum Puddin' says, "It's amazing to walk in the area Jesus actually set foot on."

"We feel the same way," says Jewel and Shalome.

They keep walking and come to a hill and Hirsh says, "This hill is called, Golgotha, meaning, "The place of the Skull." It's also called Calvary. This is where Jesus was crucified for our sins."

Then Tzivia says, "After Jesus was crucified, He was laid in a tomb that is not far from here, by a man named of Joseph of Arimathea. After Jesus was buried, a stone was rolled in front of His tomb. Then, three days later, He rose again and was seen by many of His followers. During His time on earth, Jesus invited many to ask Him to come into their hearts."

Then Shalome says, "He also said that He was going back to Heaven to prepare mansions for those who asked Him to come into their hearts and lives. Before He left, Jesus said He would come back again, so we are waiting for either us to go to Him when we die or for Him to come back to take us to be with Him." "

I sure do choose to follow Him," says Plum Puddin' and everyone else says yes, they choose to follow Jesus too.

"What a joy to be here in Jerusalem, where the Bible comes to life," says Snowdeer.

"Yes, it sure is," says Sandi. So, they walk the streets of Jerusalem and spread peace and good cheer to all they meet.

"Snowdeer, we have a secret we want to share with you," says Hirsh.

"What is it sir," asks Snowdeer.

Hirsh answers, "We have been friends with the Prime Minister and his wife for a long time. We love our God, our country and our Prime Minister and his family."

Then Shalome asks, "Would you like to meet them?"

"Oh, yes sir!" answers Snowdeer.

"Alright, we will go first to see them and ask them to give you clearance to come meet them. We will speak with them about you and your Mission from Santa so they will know why you are paying them a visit," says Shalome.

Then Snowdeer says, "Thank you very much! We will be here waiting for you."

So, off Shalome and Hirsh go to see the Prime Minister and his wife. When they come back, they have great news to share with Snowdeer and the gang! They tell them the Prime Minister is eager to see them and he's waiting at the Palace right now for them to come visit!

An excited Snowdeer and gang follow them to the Palace. As they go through the Palace doors, they marvel at the beautiful craftsmanship that they are sure took many years to build! They walk down a long hall that leads to the Royal Hall where the Prime Minister and his wife are waiting for them. Snowdeer and the gang bow before them

The Prime Minister says, "Shalom! My friends Shalome and Hirsh have told me all about you Snowdeer and the ambassadors with you! We want you to know you are forever welcome here! We will have a feast tomorrow night where I will get to know you better and hear more about your Mission from Santa. I will also announce before this day is over that there will be a great gathering on the grounds tomorrow afternoon where you can speak to the people and spread peace and good will to all, from your country to ours."

Snowdeer bows and say thank you to The Prime Minister for his gracious words. Then Snowdeer says, "Prime Minister, we will always be friends to you and to your country, Israel. We will gladly serve you and your people." The Prime Minister's wife says, "Thank you for your service to Jerusalem and all Israel. God bless you and your work."

The Prime Minister also thanks them and invites them to stay the night in their own guest rooms in the Palace. He also invites Snowdeer and the gang to meet for a special breakfast the next morning before they speak to the City. Then, he asks them to enjoy the rest of their day visiting Jerusalem and to come back later when they will be shown to their rooms for the night. They again bow, thank The Prime Minister and then leave the Palace to continue touring The Holy City.

The next morning, they are awakened by one of the servants to meet the Prime Minister and his wife for breakfast.

After they enjoy their meal and share their stories, the Prime Minister announces, "Today at 2pm, the people will join you in front of the Palace and I will tell the people who you are and what you are doing in Israel. Then, I want you to go down and speak with the people; and hear any concerns they may have and then report back to me." He looks at Hirsh, Tzivia, Shalome and Jewel and asks them to interpret for them.

They all bow to the King and Queen and say they would be honored to do it. So, that afternoon a great meeting is held on the grounds with thousands in attendance and all of Santa's Ambassadors are well received and loved.

That night, the Prime Minister and his wife meet with them in the great banquet hall for the feast they had been promised. During the meal, Snowdeer shares the concerns and wishes of the people with the Prime Minister and his wife, who are very patient and who take time to listen to each concern. After they have listened, they thank Snowdeer and all the gang and then the Prime Minister tells them he will address their concerns.

Then Snowdeer says, "Thank you. It is an honor to serve you."

Plum Puddin', who had been carrying the Magical Compass in his pocket, begins to feel it spinning. He quickly pulls it out and to everyone's surprise, he tells them, "Prime Minister, the Magical Compass is pointing northwest."

Purple Mouse, who is carrying the Magical Map, pulls it out and finds it showing the North Pole! Purple Mouse and Plum Puddin' light up with excitement when they realize Santa wants them to come home!

The Prime Minister asks, "What does all this mean?"

Purple Mouse answers, "Sir, the Magical Compass that Santa gave us was spinning around and then it stopped with its point headed northwest. Then, the Magical Map Santa gave us showed us the North Pole. Santa did this to let us know he wants us to come home."

The Prime Minister smiles and says, "Then, very well. Stay the night and leave in the morning. We will have breakfast together and I will invite the country to see you off. I want you to know that you have an open invitation to come back anytime; you are forever welcome."

Then his wife says, "Yes, please do come back Snowdeer. We will always love having a visit from you or any of your North Pole friends."

Snowdeer bows and says, "Thank you very much, Madam. I will be flying back again and I'll bring Christmas peace, cheer and good will to all of Jerusalem and all the rest of Israel every time I come."

After Snowdeer says that, the gang retires for the night with hearts that are looking forward to the next day when they go back to the North Pole.

46 - GOIN' BACK TO THE NORTH POLE

They wake up the next morning to a great breakfast of fresh bread, eggs, cheese, olives and all kinds of jams and butter. They have a great time with the Prime Minister and his wife and Plum Puddin' tells them about the Sugar Snow and how it will magically make them fly! The Prime Minister and his wife surprise them when they tell them they had their servants find Snowdeer's sleigh and that during the night they had built a runway ramp for them to take off on and that it was all ready at the front of the Palace with the Kingdom waiting to see them take off! Snowdeer and the gang bow to the Prime Minister and his wife and thank them for their kindness. The Prime Minister turns to one of his servants and asks him to bring out the special gift. He returns with a huge treasure chest.

The Prime Minister says, "This treasure chest is a token of my appreciation for all of you and for Santa and Mrs. Claus."

Everyone's mouths drop open when one of the servants opens the chest to show them gold, silver and precious jewels! Then, one of the servants leaves again to return with a special jar of Plum Pudding for Plum Puddin'!

The Prime Minister's wife looks at Plum Puddin' and says, "I heard you talking about how you were missing your Plum Pudding, so I had you some made. I will remember that you love it, and anytime you are back here in Jerusalem, I will make sure you will always have it!"

Plum Puddin' looks at her and says, "Thank you very much, Madam! I promise you, I will be back!"

Then, all of a sudden, the Magical Compass goes off in Plum Puddin's pocket and Plum reaches in and takes it out.

The Prime Minister asks, "What does the Magical Compass say?"

Plum Puddin' answers, "It shows we are to head northwest."

Then Purple Mouse checks his Magical Map and finds a new message Santa had written for them that said, "Come home, Mrs. Claus and I miss you. Also, please tell the Prime Minister and his wife thank you and that I will be there to see them on Christmas Eve!" Purple Mouse shares the message from Santa with the Prime Minister and his wife.

They get so excited by the personal message from Santa that they tell the gang they want to go back to the North Pole with them! Then, the Prime Minister says, "As much as I would love to go, I know I can't. Besides, my country would never believe me if I said we took a trip to the North Pole to see Santa! They would think I was meshuga!"

Everyone laughs and Snowdeer says, "Sir, please know I would be honored to take you both to the North Pole someday. Just say the word and we'll take you there!"

Then Plum Puddin' feels the Magical Compass starting to go off in his pocket again. Plum checks it and then says, "It's still pointing northwest. I think Santa made it go off again 'cause he really misses us! Well, I guess we should be going."

Everyone again thanks the Prime Minister and his wife and then they thank Hirsh, Tzivia, Fallo, Shalome, Jewel, Sandi, Linda and Susan. Susan and Fallo tell Snowdeer they also want to go to the North Pole someday.

Snowdeer gets a big smile on his face and asks the gang, "What do you think?" They all say "YEAH!" so Snowdeer says to Susan and Fallo, "Ok, jump on my friends! You're goin' back to the North Pole!"

Susan and Fallo get a shocked look on their faces, but then their faces turn to joy as they realize they will be joining the gang! They tell the Prime Minister and his wife and their family and friends goodbye, and then each one jumps on the back of a deer and gets ready for take-off!

Snowdeer jokes and says, "We gotta get home before we run out of room!" Everyone laughs and Snowdeer looks at the Sugar Snow and asks, "Are you ready to take us home to the North Pole?"

The Sugar Snow rises up and flies over to Snowdeer and says an excited, "Yes!" and then they begin lighting up and twinkling.

The Prime Minister says, "Snowdeer, thank you for blessing us and please come back soon! God bless you."

Snowdeer answers, "Thank you and God bless you too." Snowdeer gets a big grin on his face and he looks at the Sugar Snow and asks, "Would you put on a Sugar Snow Light Show for all of Jerusalem please?"

The Sugar Snow rise up and fly together in a huddle and talk to each other.

Snowdeer looks at Plum Puddin' and Purple Mouse and says, "This is gonna be a good one!"

Right after Snowdeer says that, the Sugar Snow starts twinkling in every color imaginable and then they fly all over, swirling around the Prime Minister and his wife, the servants and around the Palace. Then, they swirl around the people of the country who are watching. Lastly, they fly over to Snowdeer's sleigh and swirl around it and everyone in the sleigh and then around the deer and the riders. Then, they rise up above everyone and put on the greatest Sugar Snow Light Show Snowdeer had ever seen! Before they are done, they make themselves look like an Israeli flag with horizontal blue stripes on a white background with a blue Star of David in the center. Everyone is thrilled at the sight and gives a great cheer! Then, Snowdeer teaches the Prime Minister and his wife and everyone in the Kingdom the magic words to say to make the Sugar Snow fly them away.

The gang tells everyone goodbye and then Snowdeer asks, "Is everyone ready?" "Yes!" they all cheer. Then Snowdeer says, "Ok, everyone together, "SUGAR SNOW! SUGAR SNOW! BACK TO THE NORTH POLE WE GO!"

The Sugar Snow again swirls around the Prime Minister and his wife, Hirsh, Tzivia, Shalome, Jewel, Sandi and Linda and then swirls around the sleigh and all who are on it! Then the Sugar Snow swirls around the deer and all who are on them! And then, WHOOSH! Off they go to the North Pole!

47 - CROSSING EUROPE

As they soar high above Israel and the Mediterranean Sea, Plum Puddin' feels the Magical Compass go off again in his pocket. He takes it out and hands it to Carrot who wants to check it. After looking at it, Carrot says it shows they are to keep heading northwest. Purple Mouse takes out the Magical Map and hands it to Puddu who wants to check it. After Puddu sees where they are to go, he announces it to everyone that they will be flying over Turkey. As they keep pressing forward, they make their way across Bulgaria, then Romania, Hungary and then to Poland.

"The flying deer are sure getting a workout, aren't they?" asks Puddu.

"Yes, they sure are Puddu, and you can tell they love getting to do it," replies Snowdeer. Just after Snowdeer says that, the Magical Compass goes off again, showing them to continue going northwest.

Carrot says, "Since the Compass started going off again, it must mean we are getting close to something important," so he checks the Magical Map and it shows they are coming up to the Baltic Sea. Carrot tells everyone that they are going to be flying over water again and Fallo says, "I've only seen the Mediterranean Sea and the Dead Sea. I never dreamed our world would have so much water! Our world is so large!"

"Yes, it is Fallo. God is sure creative!" says Snowdeer.

A while later, Carrot checks the Magical Map again, and it shows they are flying over Sweden. Carrot enjoys being a navigator, and he keeps a regular check on where they are headed and then tells the gang. In a little bit, he discovers they will soon be flying over Norway, so he announces it to everyone. All of them enjoy hearing Carrot's reports about what countries and bodies of water they are flying over.

Once they start flying over Norway, Plum Puddin' grins and asks, "Have you noticed it getting cooler?"

"Yes, we all have noticed," says Susan, Fallo, Puddu and the rest of those in the sleigh, and then they laugh.

Meanwhile, up in the very front of the flying deer team, riding on Jim-Buck's back, Markey says, "Brrrr, I'm not used to this! I'm glad I have a thick coat of hair!"

"Oh, just wait 'till we get to the North Pole my friend, you're gonna need every single hair," says Jim-Buck and then the whole team laughs.

Plum Puddin' feels the Magical Compass go off again in his pocket, so he takes it out and he and Fallo watch it go round and round and then stop.

Fallo wants to tell everyone what it says, so he announces, "It's now telling us to head due north."

Carrot then looks at the Magical Map and says, "We're now in the Arctic Circle over the Arctic Ocean and next we will be at the North Pole!" "Yay!" everyone shouts, and the Sugar Snow, who heard what was said, swirls around the sleigh and the riders and makes their speed increase!

Plum Puddin' looks at Snowdeer and laughs and says, "I think the Sugar Snow is ready to get home as much as I am!"

Snowdeer says, "I know I'm ready to be home Plum. I miss Santa and Mrs. Santa and all the North Pole folks."

"And I miss Bev Elf," says Russ Elf. Then his face lights up as he gets an idea, and he asks, "Anyone want to hear some Christmas music?"

"Yes!" they all shout, and so Russ Elf goes to the Magical Music Box and cranks it, and out comes some of the most beautiful Christmas music they have ever heard!

Snowdeer thanks Russ Elf and then looks around at all his friends and says, "I am so thankful to have such great friends as you all and I can't wait to introduce all our new friends to everyone at the North Pole."

Susan looks at Snowdeer and says, "We look forward to meeting everyone at the North Pole too!" And after saying that, Markey, Puddu, and all those who are new to the North Pole shake their heads, agreeing with Susan. Then Susan says, "Snowdeer, are you sure Santa will be alright with Fallo and me coming along?"

Snowdeer laughs and answers, "Oh yes Susan, Santa won't mind at all. Matter of fact, if I know him, he already knows you and Fallo as well as Puddu and Markey are on your way!"

This thrills the new friends and Susan says, "I have done some teaching to young children and animals in Israel, and if Santa wants, I could teach at the North Pole while I am there. I also sing, so if Santa needs me to do that, I would be more than happy to help out."

Snowdeer replies, "Susan, that would be wonderful! I am sure Santa would appreciate it so much! There are a lot of elf children and animals at the North Pole, so to have you help would be perfect!"

Susan smiles and replies, "I would be honored to help anyway I can."

48 - SNOWDEER'S SNOW MOON

The Magical Compass goes off one more time, and once again it tells them to continue heading due North. Purple Mouse and Carrot look at the Magical Map and it shows that they are entering the North Pole! Carrot hops for joy and shouts, "We're Home everyone! The North Pole is down below!"

They all cheer and Snowdeer says, "Let's watch for Santa's runway, so we can land." As they get closer to the North Pole Village, they begin to see the snowy landscape with its many cottages. They see a tall radio tower that has a big lighted sign that has "CMAS" written across it. They see Bayberry Bay below with many elves skating on it, and the miles and miles of slides loaded with elf children sliding down them!

Snowdeer begins to hear something, and he says, "Listen! I think I hear Strike the Bell ringing!"

"Yes, it is him! I hear him too!" says Plum Puddin', and Purple Mouse points down below where they see their friend Strike ringing away in the middle of the Village. They laugh as they watch the people begin to notice them coming and then start racing to the runway to see them come in for a landing!

It has started getting dark by now, and Snowdeer asks the Sugar Snow if they would put on a special Sugar Snow Light Show for the North Pole Village. The Sugar Snow happily accept, and off they fly and brightly twinkle and turn an amazing variety of colors that light up the North Pole sky! The Villagers below OOOHH and AAHHH as the Sugar Snow puts on the best Light Show they ever have! They go down to the ground and spell SNOWDEER in the snow below and then go way up in the air and spell SNOWDEER again, along with making an arrow pointing up to the north in the sky.

Snowdeer can't figure out why the Sugar Snow is doing this, but then Plum Puddin' shouts, "Snowdeer! Look at the Moon!" Everyone, in the air and down below in the Village heard Plum Puddin', and they all look toward the Moon.

Then, Plum Puddin' shouts, "It's SNOWDEER'S SNOW MOON!" and everyone begins cheering! Snowdeer had totally forgotten about the Snow Moon with his image in the Moon, and he just stands in the sleigh staring at it; speechless!

49 - A WELCOME HOME PARTY FROM
SANTA & MRS. SANTA

After everyone had watched Snowdeer's Snow Moon for a while, the villagers start cheering for Snowdeer and the gang to come down. Snowdeer, Plum Puddin' and Purple Mouse look over the Village to find Santa's runway, and spot it in the middle of the Village. It is brightly lit, and at the end of the ramp is Amber, Lilly Kay and Ilsa Marie Elf with lantern lights directing them in. As they safely land on the runway, they hear Josh, Melody and Dale Elf singing a welcome song for them, and then the Mew Family sing, "The Good Mews of Christmas!" After they all get out of the sleigh and the deer are released from their harnesses, Bev Elf comes up to Russ Elf and gives him a hug.

The whole North Pole Village showed up and what a wonderful homecoming it is, except Santa and Mrs. Santa and a few others are nowhere to be seen! Snowdeer, Plum Puddin', Purple Mouse and the gang take off together and start looking around for them, and just as they reach Elf Hall, the big doors of the Hall burst open wide and out comes Santa, Mrs. Santa, Tasha Mouse, Jerry, Beth and Avery Elf!

When Santa sees Snowdeer and the gang, he lets out a big, "HO-HO-HO! Welcome Home! Come to our Party for you here at Elf Hall!" Then Santa opens the invitation to everyone saying, "Bring your partner and swing along, to the Christmas Party Square Dance Song! But first, a Gift from me and Mrs. Santa!"

Everyone watches as chutes come out of the roof and go down into barrels below filling them with all kinds of cookies, candies and special treats for everyone! The townsfolk are given big bags to put the goodies in, and they start filling them up to take inside Elf Hall to enjoy!

As they walk by Santa and Mrs. Santa, they thank them for their kindness and Santa lets out a big, "HO-HO-HO! You're Welcome!" After people have entered Elf Hall and the band has started playing, Santa and Mrs. Santa walk up to Snowdeer and all the gang. Snowdeer, Plum Puddin' and Purple Mouse start introducing the new members to Santa and Mrs. Claus.

Susan, Fallo, Puddu and Markey all say at the same time, "Santa, we hope you didn't mind us coming," to which Santa belly laughs and says, "No, No, not at all! I knew you would be coming! That was my plan all along! So, Welcome to the North Pole my friends! This will be your second home! HO-HO-HO!"

Tasha walks up to Purple Mouse and says, "Welcome Home Purple Mouse, I have missed you! Here are some cookies I've baked for you."

Purple Mouse gets a shy look on his face and begins to turn a bright purple! The gang sees it and they all begin to laugh, which makes Purple Mouse blush even more!

Then Santa looks at all the gang and says, "Thank you everyone for a job well done! There will be many more trips in the future and I couldn't have picked a better team to do the job! Then he looks at the new arrivals and he says to them, "I hope you enjoy your visit here; thank you for coming."

Mrs. Santa continues, "I welcome you too, and I want you to know you are welcome to come to Santa and my cottage anytime. We want to know you better and hear your stories of where you are from and about your trip to the North Pole! We look forward to showing you around and introducing you to everyone! I hope you enjoy cookies and hot chocolate because I'm always making them for Santa!"

They all laugh and Markey gets a funny look on his face. He has never had hot chocolate before, but he jokes saying, "I have never had hot chocolate, but since today is the first time I have ever been cold, I will definitely try it!" Then he beats his chest and gives out a big, "Whoop Whoop Whoop!"

Everyone laughs, and while Snowdeer watches him beat his chest, he all of a sudden remembers the special Treasure Chest gift from the Prime Minister of Jerusalem and he says, "Santa, I have a wonderful gift for you from the Prime Minister of Jerusalem." Then Plum Puddin' and Purple Mouse go back to Snowdeer's sleigh and return with the treasure chest. They sit it down in front of Santa and Mrs. Santa and Carrot opens it. He shows them the special gifts of gold, silver and precious jewels.

Santa and Mrs. Santa are thrilled with the gift and Santa says to them, "I will certainly visit the Prime Minister and his wife with some very special gifts at Christmas. They were very good this year! No Naughty List for them! HO-HO-HO!"

Santa's special helpers, Kaye Elf and Inez Elf, who are caretakers of Santa's museum down in his underground lair, have been watching and Kaye Elf says, "Santa, we will make sure this treasure chest is put in a special place in your museum on display for you."

Inez Elf looks at Harvey Elf and grins and then looks at Santa and says, "Yes Santa, we will put the treasure chest in the perfect place, that is, after Harvey moves it down there!" They all laugh as they see Harvey's face go from a smile to a frown!

Santa laughs and says, "Harvey, I will make sure it gets there, you don't have to do it!"

Then Harvey breaks into a big smile and says, "HA-HA-HA-HO-HO-HO! I don't have to move the trunk no more!" and they all laugh together.

It had gotten dark by now, so Taper and Tallow, Snowdeer's candle friends and guardsmen, light their wicks and lead Santa and Mrs. Santa and all the gang into Elf Hall, except Snowdeer, Plum Puddin' and Purple Mouse, who smile at each other and then look up to see Snowdeer in the Snow Moon! - **THE END**

BY RANDY PLUMMER

PLUMMER FAMILY CHRISTMAS
1961

Darrell, Rosie, Melody and Randy Plummer

Merry Christmas

Mom & Daddy,
Randy

CREDITS

Thank Y'all . . . .

Darrell & Rosie Plummer: Vintage pictures of Plummer Family
Russ Eugenio, Masters Media: Layout, editing and publishing
Justin Oller/Starlit Productions: Cover Design
Raine Clotfelter: Artist's rendering of Snowdeer © 2011 Randy Plummer
Dennis Tawes: Artist's rendering of Plum Puddin'SM © Randy Plummer
Tonya Lariviere: Artist's rendering of Purple Mouse © 2014 Randy Plummer
Tasha Dunne: Artist's rendering of Tasha Mouse © 2015 Randy Plummer
Sarah ("Starry") Martin: Artist's   rendering   of   Snowdeer   Character
   © 2018 Randy Plummer
Jeff Brandt: Artist's rendering of Plum Puddin' Productions LogoSM © Randy
   Plummer
Terrie Collins: Proofreading and inspiration

SNOWDEER® is a Registered Trademark by Randy Plummer

Made in the USA
Middletown, DE
22 September 2019